Robert Charles Winthrop

Reminiscences of Foreign Travel

A Fragment of Autobiography

Robert Charles Winthrop

Reminiscences of Foreign Travel
A Fragment of Autobiography

ISBN/EAN: 9783337009946

Printed in Europe, USA, Canada, Australia, Japan

Cover: Foto ©Raphael Reischuk / pixelio.de

More available books at **www.hansebooks.com**

REMINISCENCES

OF

FOREIGN TRAVEL.

A Fragment of Autobiography.

BY

ROBERT C. WINTHROP.

———

PRIVATELY PRINTED.

1894.

PREFATORY NOTE.

MANY of these Reminiscences were written long ago, and then laid aside for future consideration. Finding them during the past winter with other almost forgotten papers, I have occupied myself in adding to this little fragment of autobiography, in order to print it privately for my grandchildren and a few surviving friends. I am sensible that portions of it may seem egotistical, but this is the privilege of an octogenarian. At all events, the task has helped me through some of those weary hours which press with increasing heaviness upon one who is now within a few weeks of entering upon his eighty-sixth year.

ROBERT C. WINTHROP.

90 MARLBOROUGH STREET, BOSTON.
    April 19, 1894.

A FRAGMENT OF AUTOBIOGRAPHY.

A VALUED literary friend, to whom I once sent the Proceedings of the Massachusetts Historical Society on the Centennial Anniversary of the birthday of Sir Walter Scott, said to me in his note of acknowledgment, "I wish that you would prepare for publication, now, or when we have paid too high a price for knowledge, your recollections of the distinguished men of both hemispheres whom you have known." It was not the first time that such a suggestion had been made to me; but it was the first time that I seriously entertained it, and resolved to make, sooner or later, an effort to comply with it. I am by no means sure, however, that the effort is worth making, or that I shall succeed in jotting down anything worthy of remembrance. But I may at least occupy a leisure hour, from day to day, pleasantly and not unprofitably, in living over again some of the scenes through which I have passed, abroad or at home, and in bringing back to my remembrance, partly by the aid of old journals and letters, some of the eminent persons whom I have met more or less intimately, in other lands or in my own, but so few of whom I can meet again on earth.

I prefer to begin with those whom I have known in foreign countries, because they are fewer in number

and my account of them will thus be briefer; and
when I have once dealt with these, I shall feel that I
have finished one part of my story, and perhaps be
more ready to turn to the other and longer part.

Crossing the Atlantic for the first time in April, 1847,
I visited London with some peculiar advantages for
seeing the English celebrities of that day. I was a
member of Congress, and during the six or seven years
I had been at Washington I had served for a part of
the time on the Committee of Foreign Affairs. I had
thus been brought into official as well as personal
association with members of the Diplomatic Corps in
Washington, more than one of whom, without solicita-
tion, gave me letters of introduction. Mr. Webster,
too, on learning that I was going abroad, sent me
several valuable letters to friends in England; and Mr.
Everett, who had recently returned from there after a
four-years residence as our Minister in London, sent
me a number of introductions of the most desirable
character. Meantime Mr. Bancroft, who was then our
Minister in England, was a personal though not at that
time a political friend, and he was full of the kindest
attentions on my arrival.

My very first day in London was one to be marked
with white chalk. Calling without delay to see the
Lyells, whom I had known intimately in Boston while
Sir Charles was delivering his first course of Lowell
Institute Lectures,[1] he said at once to me: "I cannot
let you sit down an instant. You must go with me

---

[1] Lady Lyell was a far removed connection of mine, and we soon
resolved to shorten the distance and count ourselves cousins for life.

without a moment's delay to the Royal British Institution. FARADAY delivers the closing lecture of his course in a few minutes; and you may never have another opportunity of hearing him." So off we hurried to Albemarle Street, where we found Faraday already on the platform, just about to commence one of those charming lectures on Chemistry, or Electro-Chemistry, which gave so much delight and instruction to all who heard him. I cannot venture, after such a lapse of time, to give the precise topics of his lecture, — unhappily, I made no notes of it; but I remember well the sweetness and the power of his manner and delivery, and the exquisite ease and grace of his experiments. Tyndall, in his memoir of Faraday, says: "Taking him for all in all, I think it will be conceded that Michael Faraday was the greatest experimental philosopher the world has ever seen."

Like so many other really great men, however, he seemed to me one of the most modest and simple. Declining all distinctions and honors, and remaining, as he said he would, "plain Michael Faraday to the last," he has impressed that name upon the pages of science so deeply that it can never be effaced. Lyell introduced me to him after the lecture was over, and nothing could have been more kind or cordial than his reception of me. His whole air and address were those of one who had rather been made to feel more humble, than more proud, by his successful researches into the realms of Nature, and who was rather awed by the wonders which baffled his inquiries than intoxicated by the success of his discoveries.

Faraday had a distinguished audience that day; and I remember being introduced to Dean Milman among others, and to Dr. Edward Stanley, then Bishop of Norwich, the father of my lamented friend the Dean of Westminster. Lyell, Faraday, Milman, and Stanley were a goodly company of notables to have been personally associated with in a single hour of my first morning in London.

But though the audience was a distinguished one, it was by no means numerous. The little theatre of the British Institution was, indeed, well filled, but it could hardly accommodate more than a few hundreds; and I could not help reverting to the scene I had witnessed only a few evenings before I sailed from Boston, when I was one of fifteen hundred or two thousand persons crowding every seat and every corner of the hall of the old Masonic Temple to hear a lecture on the glaciers by Louis Agassiz. Nor did I fail to remember, before I left the British Institution, that its earliest and most effective promoter, if not its absolute founder, was a native of my own country and of my own State, — Benjamin Thompson, afterward known to all the world as Count Rumford, of whom an admirable biography has been written by my friend Dr. George E. Ellis, and published under the auspices of the American Academy of Arts and Sciences: a man whose great services — military, civil, and still more philanthropic — in Bavaria, and whose eminent contributions ·to science and the practical arts, have entitled him to a celebrity only second to that of Franklin in our own land, and not inferior to that of Tyndall or Faraday on the other side of the Atlantic. But Rumford was of another generation, and does not come within the scope of these reminiscences.

A Sunday now intervened, of which it is enough to say that I spent a large portion of it in attending a service at Westminster Abbey and in lingering among its memorials of the mighty dead.

On Monday I began to make use of my notes of introduction, and one of my earliest calls was upon Sir ROBERT PEEL. Stopping at his door in Whitehall Gardens in a somewhat shabby equipage, I remember well the peremptory tone in which I was told by his servant, in answer to my inquiry, that Sir Robert was not at home. But I remember, too, how speedily that tone was changed when I handed him my card with the note of introduction, on the back of which was written, in his own clear and well-remembered chirography, the name of Edward Everett. "Oh, Mr. Everett, — I beg pardon, sir," exclaimed the footman; "if you will wait a moment, I will take in the letter and card and see if Sir Robert may not have returned." In another minute, the welcome sound was heard, — "Sir Robert is at home, and will be very glad to see you." This great statesman, who only a year or two before had been Prime Minister, was now in retirement, — if, indeed, the position of an active and leading member of the House of Commons can ever be called retirement. But he had no other official position, and was free from the absorbing labors and overwhelming responsibilities of a Premier. The name of

Mr. Everett, for whom Sir Robert had a great regard, secured for me a reception which I could not otherwise have enjoyed, and I was soon disabused of the impression I had carried with me from hearing so often of "the proverbial coldness of Sir Robert Peel." After a few moments' conversation about Everett and about American affairs, he said to me: "You find me engaged at this moment in filling out cards," — for he was doing this with his own pen, and had a pile of them on the table at which he was sitting, — "for an exhibition of my pictures next Saturday. I must write your name on one of them, and you must come. You will find the pictures worth seeing, and, besides, you will meet many of our best artists and not a few of our most distinguished persons. But where are you going to-night? Have you been to the House of Commons? There is a debate in which you cannot fail to be interested." I told him at once that I had already made arrangements to go with Mr. Bancroft, who had kindly proposed to take me with him to the Diplomatic Box. "I am glad of that," said he; "I shall know where to find you." And so I took my leave, and proceeded on my round of visits.

At an early hour of the evening I went with Mr. Bancroft to the House of Commons, and after some preliminary business had been gone through, the Education Bill was taken up. Several of the members came out from their seats to talk with Bancroft, and one of them — Sir William Molesworth, if I remember right — took him off to their refreshment-room for a cup of tea, leaving me alone. Just then I observed

Sir Robert, who was at the farther end of the House, lifting his eye-glass and looking intently toward me. He presently rose, and marching in his somewhat deliberate and stately way the whole length of the chamber, came up and took the seat next to me which Bancroft had left. His conversation was charming, as he recalled some of the incidents of his long service in the Commons and pointed out to me the seats of some of the older glories of the House, as well as of some of those most distinguished at the moment. He had then been in Parliament almost as long as I had lived, — having been first elected in the year I was born (1809), and having served with almost all the men best known to the modern history of England, except Pitt and Fox, who died three years before he was old enough to be chosen. During the half-hour he remained at my side, several members of note had entered into the debate, among them Mr. Roebuck. But suddenly " the Right Honorable member for Edinburgh " was announced by the Speaker, when Sir Robert said quietly but quickly to me, " You must excuse me now; Macaulay has the floor, and I never fail to attend closely to what he says." And so he marched back to his seat.

A night or two afterward I was again at the House of Commons, when the debate was closed long after midnight by Lord John Russell and Sir Robert himself. Sir Robert spoke for an hour and a half in a masterly manner, fulfilling all my expectations, and impressing me deeply with his power and persuasiveness as a debater. With a clear and telling voice, and a figure of striking dignity; without studied rhetoric or flights of fancy; simple, earnest, and at times almost impassioned, — he seemed peculiarly fitted for a parliamentary leader. I know not how it may have been with him on other occasions, but on that night he exhibited hardly anything of the *hesitation* which was then one of the proverbial attributes of English speakers. His course upon the Corn Laws the year before had not only cost him his place at the head of the government, but had broken up his party and made many of his old friends look coldly and even angrily at him. But he bore himself as bravely as if he were still the idol of the hour, and commanded the unbroken attention of a crowded house.

On the Saturday following, I was at the exhibition of Sir Robert's pictures, and found him surrounded with all that was most distinguished in art or science, in literature, in the Church, and in the State. There were Landseer and Leslie and Turner and Sir William Ross, and Eastlake and Stansfield and Westmacott. There were Hallam and Rogers and Faraday and Buckland and Dickens; there were Bunsen and Bancroft of the diplomatic corps, and Lord John Russell and Sir James Graham, and the Duke of Cambridge and the great Duke of Wellington, and I know not how many more celebrated men. And there on the walls were Sir Joshua's Dr. Johnson, and Rubens's Chapeau de Paille, and a wonderful Hobbema, and an exquisite Cuyp, and Backhuysens and Vanderveldes and Wouvermans and Gerard Douws and Metzus and Mieris and Jan Steens, until one's eye ached from gazing intently on brilliant color and beautiful design, and sought relief in the pleasant chat of those who were fairer even than the pictures, — for not a few brilliant women were of the party. The pictures, too, I was to see again a fortnight afterwards at a party given to Sir Harry Smith, the hero of Scinde, who had just returned home; and they were not less beautiful by candle-light than by daylight. Sir Robert had invited me to dine at the banquet which preceded this evening party, and soon afterwards also sent me a card for the annual dinner of the Royal Academy; but engagements prevented me from accepting either invitation, and I left London never to meet him again. It was only three years afterward that he fell from his horse on Constitution Hill, and died at only sixty-two, leaving a name which will be associated with as fine an example of pure and Christian statesmanship as has ever adorned the history of his country.

The day after my first call on Sir Robert Peel I drove to Apsley House, and left a parcel and note, with which Mr. Everett had intrusted me, for the Duke of WELLINGTON, leaving my own card also, as the Duke had gone to the Horse Guards. The same evening Lord St. Germans took me to the House of Lords, and as he took care to be there before the Lord Chancellor had taken his seat on the woolsack, he introduced me to some distinguished peers, and among others to the great Duke. On my name being mentioned to him, he replied: "Oh, yes, Mr. Winthrop, you did me the favor to bring me a note and parcel from my friend Everett. You must come and dine with me. Will you come to-morrow and meet the Directors of the Ancient Music, and go to the concert with us?" The Duke, as is well known, had a passion for ancient music, and indeed for music of all kinds. His father, the Earl of Mornington, was a composer, and several of his compositions are to be found among the chants and hymns of the Church of England. The Duke himself composed at least one chant, which I have often heard sung at Trinity Church, Boston. The Ancient Music Association was one of the oldest musical institutions in London, and its directors at that time included Prince Albert as well as the Duke of Wellington and others of the nobility. The directors were accustomed to dine at one another's houses, and proceed thence to the concert-hall. That night they were to dine with the Duke. But, alas! a dinner-party had been made for me on that same evening by Lord Morpeth, afterward seventh Earl of Carlisle, whom I had known at Washington, and who had asked me to fix the day; and I was not yet familiar enough with English etiquette to understand that the Duke's invitations, like those of royalty, were considered as commands, or at least as supplying ample apologies for breaking previous engagements. And so, in the simplicity of my heart, I told the Duke that Lord Morpeth had made a dinner for me that evening, from which I could hardly excuse myself. He took it most amiably, and added, "Well, we must fix another time." The death of his brother, Lord Cowley, was announced from Paris not long after, and he suspended all ceremonious company. But if I lost my dinner with the Duke, I tried at least to console myself by the reflection that I was probably one of the few Americans — if not the only one — who had ever had the opportunity to decline to dine with him.

It was not the only dinner which I regretted being obliged to decline during that visit to London. Sir Robert Peel's invitation to meet the Royal Academy, Bunsen's to meet the Royal Literary Fund Society, Sir John Herschel's to meet the Royal Astronomical Society, and the Duke of Richmond's to meet the Royal Agricultural Society, come back at times to my memory among lost opportunities, resulting from the most provoking conflicts of engagements. But that lost dinner at the Duke's was my first and deepest disappointment.

A few evenings later, however (Monday, April 26), I had an ample compensation. With an admission to stand on the steps of the throne, I heard the Duke make one of the best and most memorable speeches of his life. The debate was on permanent or limited enlistments in the army. Several old generals participated, as experts, in the debate, — Lord Strafford, Lord Combermere, the Duke of Richmond, and others who had distinguished themselves on the Peninsula or at Waterloo. Lord Grey, Lord Lansdowne, Lord Stanley, and Lord Brougham, too, were all earnest and eloquent in the discussion, on one side or the other. But when the Duke rose from his seat on the cross-benches, there was a silence which no one else had commanded. In a full suit of black, with his habitual white cravat fastened behind with a shining silver clasp, made conspicuous by the stoop of old age, and with hair as white as the cravat and as shining as the silver clasp, without gesture, without studied grace of attitude or of elocution, he made every word tell like a shot from a cannon. Beginning with a simple expression of his desire and determination to support her Majesty's Government, and, as her Majesty's Government (for this was a favorite phrase of his) had introduced it, to support this bill, — he proceeded to speak in the most interesting and most emphatic manner of the importance of retaining old soldiers in the army. He described some particular triumph which had recently been achieved in India, and then said: "I ask you, my Lords, whether such a feat could have been performed under such circumstances except by old soldiers. It would have been impossible. Bear in mind," he continued, "the conduct of the Emperor Napoleon with respect to old soldiers; remember the manner in which he employed them; recollect, too, how much they are prized by every Power all over the world, — and then I will once more entreat your Lordships never to consent to any measure which would deprive her Majesty's service of old and experienced men; and thus pave the way for disasters which assuredly would follow when the army should come to be employed in war."

So powerful was this plea for old soldiers, coming from the lips of the hero of so many battles, that the Duke came very near overturning the measure he had proposed to vote for. The bill would have been in jeopardy (to say the least) had not an amendment

been introduced allowing the re-enlistment of the
ten-years men, and counting their back service toward
establishing their right to a pension.

No scene in either branch of Parliament could have
been so interesting as that of the aged Duke, thus
pleading the cause of old soldiers and citing the example of the great Emperor whom he had defeated at
Waterloo. It was said at the time to be one of the
best and longest speeches he had ever made, and I
was congratulated on having happened to hear it.
I certainly congratulated myself.

It was once common to hear the Duke of Wellington spoken of as a mere soldier. I remember how
emphatically Daniel Webster repelled this idea at
my father's dinner-table, more than sixty years ago,
when the Duke had just been made Prime Minister.
"A mere soldier!" said Webster; "there's no abler
diplomatist or statesman living than Arthur, Duke
of Wellington. He makes no pretensions to being
an orator, but both his written despatches and his
reported speeches prove him adequate to every emergency of peace as well as of war; and there is no
man in England more capable of conducting the
affairs of government with wisdom and efficiency."

Walter Scott expressed the same opinion, after
meeting the Duke in Paris in 1815, declaring him
" a great soldier and a great statesman, — the greatest
of each;" and saying of him very nearly what Erskine
wrote to Washington, that he was the only man in
whose presence he was awed and abashed.

Before I left London, I had not only dined in

company with him at Lord Ashburton's, and conversed
with him for some minutes at the Queen's Ball, but
had spent an hour at Apsley House, where he had
kindly made an appointment with a lady whose great
benefactions subsequently led the Queen to adorn
the peerage with her name, to receive her, with one
other friend and myself, and show us the Waterloo
Gallery in person.

The Duke received Miss Burdett-Coutts at the
carriage door; and under his lead we passed up the
grand staircase, with Canova's heroic statue of Napoleon at its foot, and proceeded through the rooms.
We had even a glimpse of the one with the little
iron bedstead on which the Duke habitually slept, —
giving as a reason why he had adopted a bed not big
enough for any one to turn himself on, that when a
man begins to turn at all in bed, it is time for him to
turn out.

On some of the walls we saw several portraits of
Napoleon at different stages of his career, but I think
not one of the Duke himself. A new picture had
recently been sent to him by I forget what artist,
and it was still lying on the floor. "That's *his*
idea," said the Duke, " of the battle of Waterloo."
And then pointing to a portrait by Sir Thomas
Lawrence, I believe, he said : "You see that portrait
which has been injured on the corner. It is the
first Lady Lyndhurst, who was very handsome. The
mob once threw stones at me through the windows,
but they only hurt the pictures." And then he
showed us the iron shutters which he had put up for

protecting himself and his pictures in future, and which he never would allow to be removed as long as he lived. He had a charming arrangement, too, of sliding mirrors over the windows of his grand drawing-room, so as to render it more brilliant at night; but his aged arm not being quite equal to this effort, he appealed to me to aid him in exhibiting this contrivance to the ladies. After pointing out to us several large paintings, he quietly remarked, "They are only copies, however; I returned the originals to the Spanish government.[1] Here is one small original, though, which is very charming," said he. "Joseph Bonaparte carried it about with him in his carriage at Vittoria, and I had the good fortune to find it there after he had fled." And then he showed us a recent bust of his beautiful daughter-in-law, the Marchioness of Douro (now Duchess Dowager of Wellington), and pointed out with a pencil, which I feared would leave its mark upon the marble, exactly where it failed to do full justice to the original. Still again, he showed us the equestrian statuettes of Napoleon and himself in silver by Count d'Orsay, and commented critically on their execution. Finally, he took us into his *sanctum*, — his working-room, — where his despatch boxes and his books were piled up in every direction. The carpenters were engaged at the very moment in putting up new fixtures. "You see," said he, "I am obliged to have

---

[1] An unscrupulous man might have retained them, as, though Spanish property, they had been stolen by the French and then captured by the Duke.

more shelves for all these huge Parliamentary Reports. They will soon *outfolio* us out of our houses and homes." I had never heard that most significant phrase before; I could not find it in any dictionary. It may have been used then for the first time; at any rate, it came naturally and characteristically from one who had known so well how to *outflank* his enemies.

Before leaving the room, the Duke said to Miss Burdett-Coutts, "What are you going to do with your opera-box this evening?" She replied that it would be entirely at his service, as she was going into the country. "Then write me an order for it at my desk, if you please." It was while she was writing this order, that relying on the Duke's being a little deaf, I whispered to her that if I were not afraid of annoying him I would ask the Duke to write his name for me, while she was writing her name for him. "What's that you were saying?" he exclaimed; and on my confession, he added, "With all my heart," and proceeded to write "Wellington" for me on a scrap of paper, dated May 29, 1847.

Five years later the Duke died, and England was mourning for him almost at the same moment at which we were mourning for Webster.

In the years 1824–25 (while I was in college), four young Englishmen visited the United States together, all of whom had distinguished careers, and one of whom became Prime Minister. They were EDWARD STANLEY, then Mr. Stanley, afterward Lord Stanley, and ultimately fourteenth Earl of Derby; HENRY

LABOUCHERE, afterward Lord Taunton; JOHN STUART-WORTLEY, afterward second Lord Wharncliffe; and JOHN EVELYN DENISON, afterward Speaker of the House of Commons and Viscount Ossington. Webster, who knew them all, as I subsequently did, had given me letters to Denison and Lord Stanley; and I had hardly returned from leaving my letter and card at the latter's house in St. James Square before a note reached me from him, expressing his great regard for Mr. Webster, and fixing an evening for my dining with him. It was one of my first ceremonious banquets in London, and I can recall the name of no one present, except myself, who did not rejoice in some title of nobility. The Duke of Richmond, the Marquis of Exeter, the Earl of Desart with his then young and beautiful countess, Lord Redesdale, and others, made up a good representation of the Conservative party. As I was the only Commoner, my turn came last in going down to dinner; but I found a seat reserved for me next to the Duke of Richmond and Lady Stanley, and I could not have been more agreeably placed. Before the ladies had retired, Lord Stanley called to me across the table to inquire whether I had heard lately from his friend Webster, and asked me to join him in drinking the latter's health. This was the best introduction I could have had to the rest, and secured me cordial attentions.

A few evenings afterward, I heard Stanley speak for more than an hour in the House of Lords, and was fully able to understand and appreciate the great celebrity he had acquired as an orator. Few English

2

statesmen, indeed, had enjoyed greater celebrity for
eloquence, at so early an age, while he was in the
House of Commons. When I heard him first, he was
by no means old ; but sharp and severe attacks of the
hereditary malady of so many old English families
had somewhat subdued his fiery tone, and the House
of Peers was not altogether a field for the Hotspur
quality which he had exhibited in the Commons or on
the hustings. But there was a rich melody in his
tones, and a faultless finish in his phrases and periods,
and a masterly arrangement and treatment of his
topics, which commanded the deepest attention and
admiration. I heard him thirteen years, and again
nearly twenty years, afterward, when the fire was
burning still lower, and within a twelvemonth of his
death. But his singular charm of tone and thought
and illustration and manner were still unimpaired.

He was a fine classical scholar; and the translation
into English blank verse of Homer's Iliad, published
by him a few years before his death, and which had
been the diversion of his leisure hours, will secure him
an enviable remembrance in literary history. The late
George Ticknor, no mean critic, said to me one day,
"Have you read Lord Derby's Homer?" And on my
replying that I was reading it at the moment, he continued : "Well, I have read almost the whole of it, and
have compared the most noted passages both with the
original Greek, and with Pope and Chapman and other
translators, and I like it better than any. I do not
believe Wordsworth could have done it so well, if he
had tried ; and some of the most striking passages seem

to me rendered just as Milton himself would have rendered them had he undertaken the work." Not long after, I asked an eminent Greek professor of Harvard University (Sophocles) whether he had read it, and he replied: "Every word of it, and I think it the most faithful to the original of all the English translations." Such tributes — one from a master in English, and the other from a master in Greek — make up a judgment which can hardly be appealed from or reversed.

Lord Derby died at only seventy years of age, in 1869, leaving a son, the recently deceased fifteenth earl of that name, who more than once discharged the duties of Secretary of State for Foreign Affairs with signal ability, and who, with more than his father's practical wisdom, though with less of his eloquence, added new lustre to a historic title. I saw much of him during a visit he paid to Washington when I was Speaker. In later years I was repeatedly his guest in London, and he sometimes favored me with letters upon public affairs.

I had no letter to Lord BROUGHAM, but no one could be a week in London society without seeing him, or a night in the House of Lords without hearing him. I may add, that no one who had ever seen or ever heard him would be in any danger of forgetting how he looked or how he spoke. That peculiar "Paul Pry" figure and physiognomy, that upturned feature ever on the scent of something, that quick nervous gait with the glaring stripes on his habitual trousers, could never be mistaken. I met him twice at the table of Lord Lyndhurst, on two successive visits to England at an interval of nearly thirteen years, but the lapse of time had left its mark upon everything and everybody except Brougham. He was the same restless, inquisitive, loquacious, almost garrulous, person in 1860 as in 1847, full of experience, full of information, full of ambition, eager for applause, eager for controversy, never weary of work, never tired of talk, and of whom it might be doubted whether he was most anxious to shine in social or in public life, — as a statesman, or as a ladies' man.

I heard him make a long and eloquent speech on the limitation by statute of the hours of labor to ten hours, or it may have been to eight hours. In the course of it he alluded to the condition and example of the United States; and as he pronounced the name of our country, he paused for an instant and gathered himself up for one of those long and involved parentheses in which he delighted to indulge, and which he began somewhat as follows: "The United States, my Lords, — a country for which I once had some respect, and of which I should be glad, if it were in my power, to speak respectfully at this moment, but which has so outraged the sense of the civilized world by" — I forget by what, but it was undoubtedly by something connected with the Mexican War, which was then raging, or with the annexation of Texas, or with the toleration of slavery.

So violent was his tone toward this country, that one or two peers present to whom I was personally

known and by whom I was recognized, — the late Lord
Clarendon for one, — expressed to me a deep regret
that I should have been there to hear such an out-
break, but then added that there was a meaning to
it which I ought to understand. He proceeded to
tell me that a beautiful American lady, for whom
Brougham had a special admiration, had promised to
come down to the House of Lords that evening to hear
him speak, and that he had waited a considerable time
to conduct her to the ladies' gallery; but a headache
or other indisposition had prevented her from coming,
and so Brougham had vented his impatience and
disappointment in this parenthetical attack upon her
country. The lady, not having been there to hear it,
— indeed, there would have been nothing of the sort
to hear had she been able to keep her appointment,
— was probably never aware how severe an attack
her beauty and her headache conjoined had cost her
country.

But Lord Brougham's bark was ever worse than his
bite. These impetuous sallies of severity and sarcasm
were really only parentheses in the powerful and brilliant speeches of this remarkable orator, whose eloquence both at the bar and in the two Houses of Parliament, during a long term of years, was hardly
inferior to that of any man of his time.

Nor was his eloquence confined only to public places
and occasions. He had few equals for that conversa-
tional wit, humor, anecdote, and off-hand repartee
which are the life of a dinner-table. I recall a dinner-
party given by Miss Burdett-Coutts on the day on

which she had laid the corner-stone of the beautiful
church built by her in the district associated with her
father Sir Francis Burdett's parliamentary service, and
as a memorial of his labors, — when Lord Dundonald,
who had just been restored to the honors of which he
had been unjustly deprived, and Lord Brougham,
and many others of her father's old friends were
assembled around her; and when the brilliancy of the
feast and of the company was quite eclipsed by the
scintillations and coruscations of Brougham's wit and
anecdote. I dare not attempt to describe them.

Nor was Lord Brougham by any means unwilling to
recognize a great American example, when an opportunity offered itself. There is no nobler tribute to the
pre-eminent glory of Washington than that sentence
of Brougham's, which he repeated in the same precise words on two separate occasions, ten or twelve
years apart: "It will be the duty of the historian
and the sage in all ages to let no occasion pass of
commemorating this illustrious man; and, until time
shall be no more, will a test of the progress which
our race has made in wisdom and virtue be derived
from the veneration paid to the immortal name of
Washington."

I was dining in company with him in 1860, just after
he had repeated in an address at the University of
Edinburgh this memorable sentence, which I had
quoted from him twelve years before in laying the
corner-stone of the National Monument to Washington;
and I ventured to allude to the repetition, and to my
having had such good reason for remembering the

sentence. He said at once that he was proud to have the sentence remembered by an American, and that he had used it twice designedly, in the same precise words, as an evidence that it was his deliberate judgment on Washington's career and character. So we agreed to exchange addresses; and the next day he sent me not only his Edinburgh discourse, but a volume also of "Tracts, Mathematical and Physical," which he had just published, with an autograph inscription.

Of Lord LYNDHURST, — an American by birth, as is well known, — I can recall but little beyond what I said in announcing his death to the Massachusetts Historical Society, of which he was an Honorary Member. It is all printed in their Proceedings for November, 1863, and in the second volume of my Addresses and Speeches. A sentence or two will suffice for these reminiscences : —

"He was one of the few parliamentary orators, of late years, who commanded attention beyond the limits of his own land, and whose speeches, on foreign and domestic questions alike, were read with interest and eagerness in all parts of the world. There are those here who remember well how emphatically Mr. Webster spoke, on his return from England many years ago, of the clearness, cogency, and true eloquence which characterized a speech of Lyndhurst's which he himself had been fortunate enough to hear. Like Webster, he was especially remarkable for the power and precision with which he stated his case, and for the lucid order in which he arranged and argued it. His advancing

age seemed only to add mellowness and richness to
his eloquence, while it greatly enhanced the interest with which he was listened to. As late as 1860,
when he was on the verge of his eighty-ninth year,
he made a speech on the respective rights of the
two Houses of Parliament, which was regarded as
a model of argument and oratory, and which made
London ring anew with admiration of 'the old man
eloquent.'

" No one who has enjoyed his hospitality will soon
forget his genial and charming manners, and the almost
boyish gayety and glee with which he entered into the
amusements of the hour. The last time I saw him,
less than four years ago, he rose from his own dinner-
table, and placing one arm on the shoulder of our
accomplished associate, Mr. Motley, and the other on
my own, he proceeded toward the drawing-room, —
remarking playfully, as he went, that he believed he
could always rely safely on the support of his fellow-
Bostonians. . . . Living to the great age of nearly
ninety-two years, with almost unimpaired faculties,
taking a lively and personal interest to the end both
in public affairs and in social enjoyments, and dying at
last the senior peer of England, — his name and fame
will not soon be forgotten. It may safely be said, that
Boston has given birth to but few men — perhaps
only to one other, *Franklin* — who will have secured
a more permanent or prominent place in the world's
history."

Boston certainly may be proud of having given a
Lord Chancellor to England. Lyndhurst held that
high office three times.

I cannot remember whether my introduction to SAMUEL ROGERS, the poet, in connection with whom, as the author of the " Pleasures of Memory," nothing ought to be forgotten, was from Webster or Everett; but he did full honor to whichever it was, by calling at once and offering me the kindest attentions. Nothing could be more characteristic than one of his first notes to me : —

MY DEAR MR. WINTHROP, — Pray, pray come and breakfast with me at quarter before 10, any morning or every morning.

Yours ever,   S. ROGERS.[1]

And so I breakfasted with him repeatedly, — twice, absolutely alone; more frequently with five or six others.

One great advantage to a stranger in breakfasting with Rogers alone was this: he could tell over again his oldest and best stories, with the assurance that they had not been heard before. In a mixed party, on the other hand, one or more persons were certain to have heard them previously, and this restrained and disconcerted him.

At one of these *tête-à-têtes*, I remember that he dwelt almost entirely on the Duke of Wellington. He told me that many years before, when he was dining in company with the great English hero, the Duke said: " I wonder why it is that nobody ever invites me to dine on Sundays. I get three or four invitations for every other day of the week; but on Sunday, after

---

[1] There was no date to this note.

going to church [for the Duke was a regular attendant
on public worship], I have only a late lonely dinner at
home, and a desolate evening." As soon as Rogers
reached home, he sat down and wrote two or three invitations on this wise: —

"Mr. Rogers requests the honor of the Duke of Wellington's company at dinner on Sunday next, at 7½ o'clock."

"Mr. Rogers requests the honor of the Duke of Wellington's company on Sunday week [giving the date of the following Sunday], at 7½ o'clock."

Sending them both together to Apsley House, an
affirmative answer to both was received without delay;
and the Duke dined habitually with Rogers for many
Sundays in succession during that season, and perhaps
during more than one season.

Rogers took care to avoid introducing strangers or
ceremonious company to these dinners, — asking only
two or three of the particular friends of the Duke, so
that he should converse entirely without constraint.
Of these conversations Rogers made careful record;
and on one of the mornings I was with him alone, he
sent his confidential servant upstairs for his journals
of that period, and read to me many interesting passages from them, particularly one of the Duke's account
of his resigning his post in 1830, "rather," as he said,
"than be the head of a faction." This was about the
time of his greatest unpopularity, when his windows
were broken by the mob. Rogers ended by telling me
what I could not have imagined before, that the Duke
never saw Napoleon Bonaparte. He may have brought

the focus of his field-glass to bear upon him, in looking at some group at Waterloo, but he never consciously saw the Emperor.

I remember well, too, Rogers's reading to me at length, as the most striking scene he had ever met with in the records of real life, the account of Colonel the Hon. Frederick Ponsonby's sufferings on the field of Waterloo, as given in a little work called " A Voice from Waterloo," by Sergeant-Major Cotton. I bought this book from the Sergeant-Major himself at Mo..t St. Jean soon afterward, while he was guiding me over the field of the battle. The account of Colonel Ponsonby is found at page 244, and is as follows : —

" Colonel Ponsonby, of the 12th Lt. Dragoons, gives the following account of himself on being wounded. He says : ' In the *mêlée* [thick of the fight] I was almost instantly disabled in both my arms, losing first my sword, and then my rein ; and followed by a few of my men who were presently cut down, no quarter being asked or given, I was carried along by my horse, till receiving a blow from a sabre, I fell senseless on my face to the ground. Recovering, I raised myself a little to look round, being at that time in a condition to get up and run away, when a lancer passing by cried out, " Tu n'es pas mort, coquin !" and struck his lance through my back. My head dropped, the blood gushed into my mouth, a difficulty of breathing came on, and I thought all was over. Not long after, a skirmisher stopped to plunder me, threatening my life. I directed him to a small side-pocket, in which he found three dollars, all I had ; but he continued to threaten, tearing open my waistcoat, and leaving me in a very uneasy posture.

" ' But he was no sooner gone, than an officer bringing up some troops, and happening to halt where I lay, stooped down, and addressing me, said he feared I was badly wounded. I answered that I was, and expressed a wish to be moved to the rear. He said it was against orders to remove even their own men; but that if they gained the day (and he understood that the Duke of Wellington was killed, and that six of our battalions had surrendered), every attention in his power should be shown me. I complained of thirst, and he held his brandy bottle to my lips, directing one of his soldiers to lay me straight on my side, and place a knapsack under my head. They then passed on into action, soon perhaps to want, though not to receive, the same assistance; and I shall never know to whose generosity I was indebted, as I believe, for my life. By and by, another skirmisher came up, a fine young man, loading and firing. He knelt down and fired over me many times, conversing with me very gayly all the while. At last he ran off, saying, "Vous serez bien aise d'apprendre que nous allons retirer. Bon jour, mon ami." It was dusk when two squadrons of Prussian cavalry crossed the valley in full trot, lifting me from the ground and tumbling me about cruelly. The battle was now over, and the groans of the wounded all around me became more audible. I thought the night never would end. About this time I found a soldier lying across my legs, and his weight, his convulsive motions, his noises, and the air issuing through a wound in his side distressed me greatly, — the last circumstance most of all, as I had a wound of the same nature myself. It was not a dark night, and the Prussians were wandering about to plunder. Many of them stopped to look at me as they passed; at last one of them stopped to examine me. I told him that I was a British officer, and had been already plundered. He did not, however, desist, and pulled me about roughly. An hour before midnight I saw a man in an English uniform coming toward me; he was, I suspected, on the same errand. I spoke instantly, telling him who I was. He belonged to the 40th, and he had missed his regiment. He released me from the dying soldier, and took up a sword and stood over me as a sentinel. Day broke, and at six o'clock in the morning a messenger was sent to Hervé; a cart came for me, and I was conveyed to the village of Waterloo, and laid in the bed, as I afterward understood, from which Gordon had but just before been carried out. I had received seven wounds; a surgeon slept in my room, and I was saved by excessive bleeding.'"

It may be conceived that I "supped full of horrors," or rather breakfasted, in hearing this thrilling account from the sepulchral voice of the old poet.

At another of these breakfasts I met Milman, the Dean of St. Paul's; Whewell, the well-known Master of Trinity; Thirlwall, Bishop of St. David's and historian of Greece, and Lord Glenelg, a former Secretary of State for the Colonies, — among whom a discussion arose as to what, upon the whole, was the best *story* ever written. The unanimous voice was for Goldsmith's "Vicar of Wakefield;" and on a further inquiry as to the next best, the general judgment, to my great surprise, for I could not then remember that I had ever read it, was in favor of Mrs. Inchbald's "Simple Story." It happened that in Paris, not long afterwards, I picked up a volume of "Baudry's European Library," containing only these two stories bound together. I bought it at once, and wrote this judgment of these London wits on the fly-leaf, as a souvenir of the occasion.

At still another of these breakfasts I met only ladies, — the Countess of Orford and her daughter Lady Dorothy Walpole, since better known as Lady Dorothy Nevill, the Dowager Lady Lyttleton, Mrs. Leicester Stanhope, afterward Countess of Harrington, and Lady Bulwer-Lytton. This was on the 17th of July, accord-

ing to my journal; and Rogers is said in the Biographi-
cal Dictionaries to have been born on the 31st, a fortnight
later. But the occasion was certainly alluded to as
Rogers's birthday festival, — his eighty-fourth, — and
Lady Bulwer-Lytton took from her bosom an original
ode for the occasion, which she read to him aloud. I
remember, too, his telling me that he had a journal of
sixty-seven years ago, recording a dinner in Paris (at
which he was present) of twelve persons, I think, all
but two or three of whom had afterward died violent
deaths. This must have been at the table of Lafayette,
as in " The Table-Talk of Rogers," published after his
death, he speaks of his first visit to France, just before
the Revolution, as follows (page 41): —

" When we reached Paris, Lafayette gave us a general invitation to dine with him every day. At his table we once
dined with about a dozen persons (among them the Duc de
la Rochefoucauld, Condorcet, etc.) most of whom afterward
came to an untimely end."

Rogers must ever be remembered kindly by Americans, were it only for the anecdote he was so fond of
recalling of his father, who, on hearing of the first·blood
shed at Lexington, — he himself remembered it as a
boy of twelve years old, — put on a full suit of black,
and afterward wore nothing but mourning colors until
his death. He sent me a beautiful copy of his works,
in two volumes, with an autograph inscription, before
I left England, and on my return home I ventured to
recall myself to his remembrance by sending him a
little essay on " Health " by my brother-in-law, the late
Dr. John C. Warren, together with two of my own

addresses and speeches, — one of them, that in which as Speaker of the House of Representatives of the United States I had announced the death of Ex-President John Quincy Adams.

His acknowledgment is too characteristic to be omitted from these reminiscences: —

LONDON, April 20, 1848.

MY DEAR MR. WINTHROP, — Recall yourself to my remembrance is what you cannot do, for I must first forget you, and forget the many pleasant hours I have passed in your company. The first volume (on Health) I have read again and again with no less profit than pleasure, and the second who can leave till he has read it?

They would have been precious gifts, come whence they might, and I need not say how highly I shall value them on every account, for their own sake and for yours.

But are you now condemned to listen, and am I never again to hear you? Being now acquainted with your voice, I could now hear you when you spoke, and, deaf as I am, catch every syllable from your lips when it came across the Atlantic.

What strange events are now passing in the Old World! May they not extend to the New!

Yours with great regard,

SAMUEL ROGERS.

A thousand thanks for your very affecting address in Congress. J. Q. A. has sat with me more than once as my guest at the very table on which I am now writing.

Rogers has often been called surly and cynical, and he certainly knew how to show his teeth on occasions. He liked to say striking, epigrammatic things. One morning Chester Harding, our well-remembered portrait painter, called on me in London and said: "I am taking a portrait of Rogers, and he is to give me a sitting to-day. I want you, and he wants you, to come and keep him company while I am painting him." An inexorable engagement compelled me to decline the invitation. The portrait was finished, and not long afterward one of Rogers's friends said to him, "So you have been sitting to an American artist. Is it like?" "*Infernally like!*" was the only reply. Yet the picture was a good one, and quite just to the original. It was for Mr. Everett, and long adorned his library. But it is hardly surprising that with so much youth of heart, a poet should be impatient under a faithful representation of all the infirmities and wrinkles of eighty-four.

I met Rogers often at other houses besides his own. I was at luncheon with him one day at Miss Burdett-Coutts's, when the servant came in and whispered something in her ear, upon which she instantly exclaimed, "Why, Mr. Wordsworth is at the door!" "Wordsworth!" said Rogers, "he is not in London." But in another moment the great poet of the Lakes was with us at the table, and I was of course presented to him. As it happened, I had brought a letter to him from Mr. Ticknor, which I was to use on my way along the Cumberland Lakes, and on learning this he greeted me most pleasantly. While we were at table, Miss Coutts chanced to inquire after a favorite servant named James, whom she had seen at Rydal Mount. "He is with me," said Wordsworth. "With you! where?" asked Rogers. "At the door," said Wordsworth. "James at the door!" exclaimed Miss Coutts, "why, I must go and see him." "So must I," said Rogers. And thereupon the whole party hastened out to the street door in Stratton Street to greet the faithful attendant of the poet, who had won upon all their hearts by the care which he took of his aged master.

WORDSWORTH was then in his seventy-eighth year, and looked quite infirm, with a spiritual look like our Washington Allston's. He was in the first anxiety, too, for a beloved daughter, who died in a few weeks from that time, just as I was passing along Windermere with a view of calling to see her father agreeably to his request and my promise. I was unwilling to intrude upon so fresh a grief, and wrote him a note of sympathy and apology. The luncheon at Miss Burdett-Coutts's was thus my only interview with Wordsworth. He died in 1850. Ten years after his death, I was again among the Lakes, and as I was passing his house I saw a red flag at the gate, betokening an auction sale. I stopped, and found that Wordsworth's library was being sold in the barn, to which it had been removed. I went in and found quite a company of book-fanciers. I saw one parcel knocked off, but could not resist the temptation of the second parcel. I made a bid, and was successful; but on being called on for my name, I asked leave to take the books and pay for them at once, and to my consternation was refused. So I had to make a little speech in Wordsworth's barn, saying "that I was an American, accidentally passing by, and that my family were awaiting me in the rain at

3*

the door; that I had enjoyed the privilege of knowing Mr. Wordsworth personally, and desired only to obtain a souvenir of one I had so much admired." The auctioneer at last gave a surly assent, taking my money and giving me the books, but stoutly declaring that it was the only such interruption he would tolerate. So I paid my money and carried off my prize rejoicing.

The books were quite miscellaneous, and of no great intrinsic value; but almost all of them had Wordsworth's autograph, and had evidently been read by him. Indeed, one of them proved to be a book of which he had a high opinion. Crabb Robinson, in his Reminiscences, says of George Dyer: "He wrote one good book, the 'Life of Robert Robinson,' which I have heard Wordsworth mention as one of the best books of biography in the language," adding that "Dr. Samuel Parr pronounced the same opinion." This was one of the books which I purchased so accidentally in Wordsworth's barn at Rydal Mount, and it has an additional interest from its quaint calico binding. Happening to show it to Lord Houghton, when he was one day lunching with me in Boston, he told me that it was probably bound by Mrs. Southey, whose habit it was to bind her husband's books with fragments of her chintz or calico dresses, and who may have treated one of her neighbor's books to a similar covering. The volume is thus doubly redolent of the Lake poets.

Of BUCKLAND and WHEWELL and LYELL and HALLAM, all of whom I met often, and to more than one of whom I was indebted for repeated attentions, I have little except their kindness to recall. Yet I cannot omit a delightful breakfast at Hallam's at which many of them were present, and with them the late amiable Earl of Carlisle, to whom I have previously alluded as Lord Morpeth. English reserve has rarely been more strikingly illustrated than when, during this breakfast, Milman inquired across the table as follows: —

"Lyell, I am quite curious to know who it was I sat next to at breakfast yesterday at Buckland's. He was a most intelligent and agreeable person. Did you know his name?"

"No," said Lyell, "I really did not know who he was, though I was as much struck with him as you were!"

English people at that day never introduced persons to one another, and you might breakfast or dine out in the best society every day for a whole season without knowing to whom you had sat next or with whom you had been conversing. It was at this same breakfast, I think, that Lord Carlisle said to me, —

"Mr. Winthrop, did you hear Chalmers last Sunday?"

"Chalmers," I replied; "I did not dream that he was within a hundred miles of London. Where can I see or hear him?"

Alas! he had already left town, and hardly a day had elapsed before the public journals announced that he had died suddenly on his return home. I had thus lost the opportunity of hearing the last sermon in London, if not the last sermon anywhere, of that eloquent and excellent man. Among all the lost opportunities of my first visit to Europe there was hardly one which I regretted so much.

I did not fail, however, during this and other visits to England to hear and to know some of her most distinguished preachers. Webster had once told me that of all the speakers he heard in the British Parliament none impressed him so much for simplicity, clearness, directness, and force as Sir James Graham in the House of Commons, and BLOMFIELD, Bishop of London, in the House of Lords. He gave me a letter to Blomfield, and I dined with him, and was at his house more than once. I heard him make a short speech in the House of Lords and preach a good sermon at St. George's, Hanover Square. He reminded me of my own former Rector, Dr. John Sylvester John Gardiner, of Trinity Church, Boston, who was born in England and was a pupil of Dr. Parr. A fine voice, distinct articulation, and dignified manner gave a tone of authority to all he said, heightening the effect of strong sense and a classical style. He was eminently direct, as Webster said; not a word or illustration aside from the purpose.

WILBERFORCE, then Bishop of Oxford, afterward of Winchester, had far more of rhetorical grace and art. He was long the foremost orator of the bench of bishops, and it was often difficult to get a seat where it was known he was to preach. I breakfasted with him soon after my arrival in London in 1847. As he had written the history of " The American Church," and was familiar with the earliest New England annals, he more than once made it a subject of comment and of congratulation that the lineal descendants of Governor Winthrop, the Puritan, had long since got back into the Episcopal fold. When I was in England the second time, I made special application to him for a seat at the church where he was to preach, and the following characteristic note to one of the vestry or clergy of St. Peter's will tell with what result: —

26 PALL MALL, Saturday, June 9.

MY DEAR MR. FULLER, — Will you kindly send one line with order of admission for two ladies and one gentleman to-morrow, for some tip-top American friends of mine, to the Hon. Rob. Winthrop, the Albermarle Hotel?

I am most sincerely yours, S. OXON.

Of course I had an excellent seat and was greatly gratified. The sermon was a most impressive and admirable appeal for some charitable object, and afforded me a striking proof of the bishop's pulpit eloquence. But I afterward heard a still more effective utterance of his in the House of Lords of an entirely different character. It was a speech in reply to the Duke of Argyll on the disestablishment of the Irish Church. Longfellow and I were together on the steps of the throne, and were deeply impressed by the force and dignity of the Duke's speech. Wilberforce was powerful and eloquent, also; but his speech had nothing of the bishop except the lawn sleeves, and was as personal and pungent a piece of stump-speaking as we could have heard in our own land. Longfellow well said that the Duke was more like a bishop in that debate. But Wilberforce had great qualities both as a prelate and a statesman, and was a delightful companion, endeared to all who knew him. He was a younger son of the renowned and revered philanthropist William Wilberforce, whose celebrity was wide enough and enduring enough to distinguish a whole family for a dozen generations. But he early extricated himself from the often oppressive shadow of a great paternal or ancestral name, and asserted his individual title to an exalted place both in the ecclesiastical and the civil history of his country. Indeed, few prelates of the English Church, in our own day or in any other day, took a more conspicuous stand or enjoyed a wider and more deserved distinction. His successor in the See of Winchester, DR. HAROLD BROWNE, I also knew and greatly liked.

One of the most notable prelates whom I knew in 1847 was RICHARD WHATELY, Archbishop of Dublin. I met him first at a breakfast at Nassau W. Senior's, to whom Webster had given me a letter. When I entered the room, where the other guests had arrived before me, I saw a tall gaunt figure, in a straight-bodied coat, with tightly gaitered legs and an apron appended to his waistcoat, standing with his back to the fire and holding up a small puppy by the nape of its neck, upon which he was discoursing most humorously. I was hardly prepared for meeting one of the great thinkers and writers of the English Church in such an attitude. But Whately had a vein of drollery which could not be controlled, and which he did not

care to control. He was full of anecdote and witty
repartee during the breakfast, and made me quite at
home with him by his personal cordiality and kindness.
He insisted on taking me to my hotel, after breakfast
was over, in his chariot, and made me promise to come
and see him in Dublin, if I should cross over to
Ireland in the summer.

I met him next at a big dinner at the Marquis of
Lansdowne's (then President of the Council), where
several Cabinet ministers were present. It was pleasant
and sumptuous, but had a little of the coldness and for-
mality which might be imagined in a banquet hall
almost lined with antique marble statues. Whately,
however, did not fail to " set the table in a roar " now
and then, until he retired with Lady Lansdowne and
the other ladies, while the gentlemen remained for half
an hour to try the qualities of the Lansdowne cellar.
When we went up to the drawing-room I found the
Archbishop, with cards and scissors in hand, lecturing
on the principle of the *boomerang*, cutting out little semi-
circular strips and blowing or snapping them so as to
make them return upon his own nose or head. He
was in great glee, and the ladies quite wild with
merriment.

When I was in Dublin, a few months afterward,
Whately accompanied me through Trinity College
and took me also to visit the National Schools of
Ireland, where Bible lessons, arranged by him and the
Roman Catholic Archbishop, were daily read. He
was specially proud of having been the means of
bringing about such a reconciliation of the Protestant

and Catholic children, so that the Bible should be read to them both. But, alas! this reconciliation was short-lived, and dissensions and jealousies soon put an end to the arrangement. The volume containing these Bible lessons is still in my possession, given me by Whately himself, and I cannot but hope that something of the same sort may be found permanently practicable on this side of the Atlantic, if not on that.

Whately gave me several other books. It happened that while I was studying law with Webster, Whately's Rhetoric had been recently printed, and Webster came into the office one morning and said: "Winthrop, have you read the essay on rhetoric by Archbishop Whately? If not, get it and read it at once. It is worth all the classics on that subject." I found an opportunity to tell this to Whately; and the next day he sent me the latest editions both of his Rhetoric and Logic, with a kind note. He sent me at the same time several copies of two separate pamphlets, in which were comprised all the alterations and additions which he had made in his new edition, begging me to give them to any persons in the United States who were interested in his works. He told me these pamphlets of "alterations and additions" were printed, at his own cost, for gratuitous distribution, as he preferred to be read correctly rather than to make money out of new editions. He complained that our publishers not only printed all his works, but did not take the pains to make the changes, — sometimes putting second or third edition on the titlepage, without any reference to the corrections or new matter which these editions contained.

Whately was proud of having so large a number of American readers, and said there was only one of his books which had not been reprinted in the United States, and of which he had not himself obtained an American edition. This was the "Essay on the Difficulties of the Writings of Saint Paul." It has been printed at Andover since his death. "If I could have," said he, "a penny a volume on all the copies of my books printed in America, I should be far richer than I ever have been from the See of Dublin." He asked me to take some of his books to Alonzo Potter, Bishop of Pennsylvania, of whom he expressed the very highest opinion, and for whom he had formed a warm friendship; and he continued to send me his pamphlets for many years after my return to America, and almost to the time of his own death.

If it be true, as has been said, that Whately became in his old age a convert to modern Spiritualism, it is only a proof how the strongest intellect and clearest perception and solidest common-sense may be betrayed by that passion for novelties which is the besetting sin of ambitious souls. He loved notoriety, and was willing to be remarked upon for eccentricity rather than not to be remarked upon at all. Yet, take him for all in all, few English prelates have contributed more to the cause of religious, moral, and intellectual advancement. I never heard him preach, but his little volumes of sermons, as a curate, on a "Future State" and on "Good and Evil Angels," show how instructive a preacher he must have been.

Whately was succeeded in the See of Dublin by
TRENCH, whom I knew while he was Dean of Westminster, and whom I heard preach in the Abbey.
Meeting Rufus Choate, so long the leader of our Boston Bar, one day in State Street, he said : "What are
you reading? Stop at Little & Brown's and get a
copy of the Hulsean Lectures by Richard Chenevix
Trench. There is nothing of late days equal to them
for richness of style and grandeur of thought." From
that time I read everything of Trench's, — prose and
poetry, sacred and secular, — the "Parables" and
"Miracles," the Essays on Words and on Proverbs, the
Life of Calderon, the poems, and first of all, of course,
the Hulsean Lectures. I thus knew him almost as well
before breakfasting at his table, and being with him an
hour in the "Jerusalem Chamber," as after enjoying
such opportunities of conversing with him personally.
His sermon at Westminster Abbey was excellent, but
not so impressive in delivery as I had anticipated. In
conversation and in books he was greater than in preach-
ing. He was a marvellous master of words and style,
and his thoughts were often powerful and his illustra-
tions brilliant; but his magnetism seemed to evaporate
before he ascended the pulpit. I remember meeting
him again at Oxford (when he took the degree of
Doctor of Laws in company with my friend George
Peabody, the philanthropist, and when I sat next to
him at the Vice-Chancellor's dinner), and again in
London, in 1874, when his health was failing.

I recall that on the other side of me at the Vice-
Chancellor's table was MANSEL, the author of the

" Limitations of Religious Thought," a profound meta-physical work, and who was afterward Dean of St. Paul's. Ardent, joyous, full of anecdote and clever repartee, Mansel seemed to have before him a long career of intellectual activity; but he had hardly succeeded Milman at St. Paul's, in less than three years after I had known him, when he was struck with apoplexy and died.

MILMAN I knew in the cloisters of Westminster Abbey in 1847, when he was a canon, and met him often at his own house and at other houses at each succeeding visit to London. Webster had given me a note to his charming wife, whom everybody admired and loved, and they were both full of kindness to me. His great historical works on Christianity and the Jews are as well known in our country as in his own. His " Martyrs of Antioch" have furnished a sweet and touching hymn for many a funeral service. His " Fazio" has supplied a character (Bianca) for Fanny Kemble's most powerful impersonation; nothing in Shakspeare gave more scope to her genius. But those who have not known him in the cloisters of Westminster or in the Deanery of St. Paul's have not known him at all. Full of information and eager to impart it, with nothing of bigotry or intolerance, quiet in manner, genial in temper, given to hospitality, he attracted the best and most accomplished men of all professions, and seemed always happy in making others happy. The last time I saw him he took me to afternoon service at the cathedral; and though his form was so bent and

bowed by infirmity that I might have feared lest each
step should be his last, his eye was as bright, and his
brow as earnest, and his voice as cheery, and his kindness as assiduous as if he were still in his prime.   He
was spared to complete "The Annals of St. Paul's,"
and to direct the execution of his cherished plans for
the restoration of the grand cathedral; and in view of
all he did in this regard, we might almost as well say
of him as of its architect, "Si monumentum quæris,
circumspice."

Two of the most interesting and valuable additions
to historical and antiquarian literature in our time are
"The Annals of St. Paul's," by Milman, and "The
Annals of Westminster Abbey," by Dean Stanley.
The name of ARTHUR PENRHYN STANLEY was early
known in this country as well as in England by his
admirable life of his great master, Dr. Thomas Arnold
of Rugby, — a name never to be pronounced without
respect and almost veneration, but a name hardly ever
heard of out of England until Stanley introduced it
to us and won for himself the honor of an able and
faithful biographer of a really great and good man.
Stanley subsequently added many new claims to the
consideration and respect of the literary and religious
world.   His " Sinai and Palestine," his " Memorials of
Canterbury," and his lectures on the Jewish Church,
as well as his " Annals of Westminster Abbey," have
been read and highly valued on both sides of the
Atlantic; while his liberal views, and the independence
with which he advocated them, deservedly made him a

leader of advanced thought in the Church. He seemed to me peculiarly an apostle of Christian fraternity, — of that brotherly love which has so happily supplanted the *odium theologicum* of former times.

Meeting him first at a breakfast at Trench's in 1860, I had frequent opportunities from that time until his death, alike at his house, in my own, and elsewhere, to appreciate the exceeding charm of his personal intercourse. I had the good fortune once to be present at Westminster Abbey when he delivered a memorable sermon, prompted by three events of no little interest at least to Englishmen, — the thirtieth anniversary of the Queen's coronation; the escape of the Duke of Edinburgh from an attempted assassination; and the safe return of Lord Napier of Magdala and his army from their brief but decisive campaign in Abyssinia. The Abbey was crowded. The Prince and Princess of Wales and many others of the royal family were present. The choral service was brilliant, and the grand organ thundered forth the National Anthem most impressively. The slight figure, quiet manner, and simple style of the preacher were in striking contrast with the surroundings, and furnished welcome proof that he was incapable of being betrayed into any mere sensational rhetoric, or of being diverted from a plain, practical enforcement of the moral and religious lessons of the hour. He felt, and made others feel, that he was speaking in the presence and as the servant of One above all earthly heroes or princes.

The recent admirable life of him by Dean Bradley

and Mr. Prothero cannot fail to enhance the affection-
ate veneration with which his memory will henceforth
be regarded by all who are capable of properly appreciating his exalted character. A somewhat elaborate
tribute which I paid him at the time of his death is to
be found in the fourth volume of my Addresses and
Speeches, and I resist the temptation to reprint passages from it here. I always remember with especial
pleasure my constant intercourse with him in Paris,
in 1875, when his devoted wife, Lady Augusta, was
so ill at Madame Mohl's, as well as the week he subsequently passed in my house at Brookline.

Among my English friends and correspondents there
have been none for whom I have felt a warmer personal regard than for Lord ARTHUR HERVEY, Bishop
of Bath and Wells (still, I rejoice, surviving), and the
late JOHN SINCLAIR, long Archdeacon of Middlesex
and Vicar of Kensington.

Before his elevation to the episcopate, a quarter of
a century ago, Lord Arthur held the family living
of Ickworth in Suffolk, and was for some years Archdeacon of Sudbury. Some of his lectures at the Bury
Athenæum, and some of his contributions to the published
Proceedings of the Suffolk Institute of Archæology, bore
testimony to his accomplishments and culture at that
period. Since then he has become widely known as
the successful administrator of an important diocese, as
the author of charges to his clergy replete with dignity and wisdom, as an influential member of the Com-
mission for Revising the Holy Scriptures, and as the

writer of a remarkable course of lectures upon the authenticity of St. Luke's Gospel. I have had repeated opportunities for appreciating the charm of his domestic circle both amid the pleasing rural scenery of Ickworth Rectory and the picturesque surroundings of the episcopal palace at Wells. It was while on a visit to him at Wells that I first met his neighbor, the historian Freeman.

Archdeacon Sinclair brought me a note of introduction when he came over with Bishop Spencer and others many years ago to attend the Triennial Convention of the Protestant Episcopal Church at New York. Almost immediately on receiving him, I ventured to inquire whether he were not a son of that Sir John Sinclair who corresponded with Washington on agriculture; and on his replying in the affirmative, I said, "I suppose you have an abundance of copies of that correspondence as printed long ago in England?" "Not one," said he; "we have given them all away from time to time, and I have not even saved a copy for myself." "Then," said I, "perhaps you will accept this copy from me," taking one from the table at my side, where I had a dozen of them which had just been sent to me as a Trustee of the Massachusetts Agricultural Society, by whom a new edition had been printed for distribution as prizes that very year. It was a striking coincidence, and amused and gratified us both. Since then I twice visited him at his pleasant vicarage of Kensington, and at least once partook the Communion from his hands in old Kensington church, which has now disappeared for a new one. Among the persons

I met at his table were two of his sisters, — Miss
Catharine Sinclair, whose writings are so well known,
and the Dowager Countess of Glasgow, — Lord Chancellor Hatherley, then Sir William Page Wood, and
others whose names have escaped me; and I owed to
him an introduction to the late Lady Holland, and
several charming visits to Holland House, as well as to
Dean Ramsay and other friends of his in Edinburgh.
There never beat in human bosom a kinder heart than
in that of the good Archdeacon. His sermons and
charges, of which he sent me not a few, were full of
good sense as well as of religious instruction. Successive bishops of London leaned on him for support.
Macaulay was one of his parishioners. Some sketches
of eminent men whom he had known, printed for
private circulation only, were excellent. Without pretensions to the graces of oratory, simple and natural
in expression and delivery, the one sermon I heard
from him was admirably adapted to a Communion
Sunday, and prepared us all for partaking in the
right spirit of that simplest, solemnest feast.

I may not forget, in this connection, that I have been
in the company of three successive Archbishops of
Canterbury. Of the earliest (SUMNER), in 1847, I saw
but little, and was only presented to him formally. Of
the two others I have happily been privileged to know
more. A delightful afternoon at Lambeth with Longfellow, accompanied by the ladies of our party, is fresh
in my memory. LONGLEY was then Primate, and a
more charming old man has rarely been seen. I had

heard him preach forcibly and eloquently ten or twelve years before in Paris, while he was Bishop of Ripon. Since then he had been Archbishop of York for a very brief term, — giving room for the *bon mot* of Punch, "Longley, Archbishop of York; Shortly, Archbishop of Canterbury." He was a favorite at Court, as he deserved to be for his piety and excellence, and the earliest opportunity was taken to make him Primate. He was full of kindness in taking us into the old Lambeth chapel and showing us where the first American bishop was consecrated; and he sent his son with us to the top of the Lollard's Tower, with its interesting historical associations, and its exquisite view of London and the Thames, the shipping and the bridges. Some of the ladies were but too well satisfied to remain below and enjoy his delightful conversation. He died soon after our return to America, universally respected and beloved.

His successor, Dr. TAIT, I had previously known as Bishop of London; and in my address at Plymouth in 1870, on the 250th Anniversary of the Landing of the Pilgrims, I was led, in speaking of the Bradford Manuscript, to give some account of visits to him at Fulham, since which time I have repeatedly been his guest at Lambeth Palace, and have been invited to stay with him at Addington. A man of the greatest simplicity of manner and character, Dr. Tait seemed to me as well calculated to win hearts to the Church and to Christ as any one I had ever known. The apparent feebleness of his health only added to his attractions, though there

was nothing feeble in his tone. Eminently prudent,
conciliatory, liberal, and wise, he seemed made for presiding over the councils of the English Church at a
moment when a stern or bigoted policy must have cost
a breach, if not a schism. I never heard him preach,
but I was present during the first debate on the Bill
for disestablishing the Irish Church, when he rose
about midnight and made one of the most admirable
and impressive speeches to which I have ever listened.
Advancing to the middle of that magnificent chamber,
crowded with all that was most distinguished in rank,
statesmanship, literature, and theology, without notes
and with no evidence of formal preparation, he dis-
cussed the policy of the bill with a moderation, a
clearness, a precision, and a power which were worthy
of his position and of the solemnity of the occasion;
and I could say of Tait, as Webster said of his
predecessor in the See of London (Blomfield), that I
heard nothing better of its kind in either House of
Parliament. His death, fourteen years later, was a
great public loss.

I must not omit to allude to my slight acquaintance,
in 1847, with the venerable Dr. VERNON-HARCOURT,
then Archbishop of York, who told me that he saw
Webster for only a few minutes, but that in that brief
interview he learned more about the American Constitution than in all the rest of his life. My own interview with him, alas, was as brief as Webster's, and
left only the impression of a grand old prelate, ripe for
the translation which he soon experienced, whose noble

monument in York Cathedral I saw on my next visit
to England. From two of his sons, both members of
the House of Commons, Colonel George Harcourt, of
Nuneham, and Granville Vernon, I received polite attentions. The former became, somewhat late in life,
the third husband of the famous Frances, Countess
Waldegrave; and the latter was the father of a charming woman, the second wife of my friend and remote
connection, Humphrey Mildmay.

Nor can I fail to recall the kindness which I received
in 1847 and afterward from the late Lord LANSDOWNE,
to whom I have already passingly alluded. He was
hardly a great statesman, but he had elements of character which are even better than greatness. Frank,
honest, cordial, genial, he was the man of all others for
a President of the Council, and seemed eminently calculated to influence the course of government by persua-
sion rather than by force; to be always ready with
conciliatory explanations, to temper and control the
extravagances of party leaders, and to preside over
public ceremonials and administer official hospitalities.
After breakfasting *tête-à-tête* with him on one occasion, he took me in his carriage to see one of the
" Home and Colonial Juvenile and Teachers' Schools "
in which he was interested, and gave me a number of
the school-books to bring home for comparison with
our own. But some of these books were really *our own*,
though not perhaps under the name of the American
author. There was a great power of appropriation, assi-
milation, and digestion among the commoner sort of

English book-makers, and they did not always give credit for what they borrowed, still less for what they stole. We have been dishonest enough in the matter of copyright, but when we reprint, we at least acknowledge the authorship to belong elsewhere.

Lord Lansdowne kindly invited me to be his guest at Bowood after the rising of Parliament, and promised me a meeting with Tom Moore; but I had then never been on the Continent, and had much to do and see before returning home for the ensuing session of Congress. I less regretted not meeting Moore as he was fast becoming a wreck, and little but the name of the charming poet and songster was left. I was similarly obliged to forego visits to Lord Ashburton at the Grange, and to Evelyn Denison at Ossington; but I found time for a pious pilgrimage (the first of several) to the home of my ancestors at Groton, in Suffolk, in which neighborhood I was hospitably entertained by RICHARD ALMACK, of Long Melford, a leading member of the Society of Antiquaries, the possessor of an exceptional store of local information, who, from that time until his death in 1875, was one of my most valued friends and correspondents. I found time, also, in the course of a flying trip through Scotland, to pass a couple of days with Webster's friend, the nineteenth Earl of MORTON, at Dalmahoy House, near Edinburgh. Lady Morton and her daughters were full of kindness; and this brief experience of Scottish hospitality caused me additional regret at having been constrained to decline an invitation from the Duke of Richmond to Gordon Castle, and from the Earl of Aberdeen to Haddo House.

Everett had given me a letter to Lord ABERDEEN, who gave a dinner for me which I came very near missing. I had ventured to go down to see the great Derby race on the same day, and found much difficulty in getting back in season, owing to the crowd. It would have been a serious loss, as the guests included Lord Canning, Sir James Graham, Lord Ashburton, Sir Robert Gordon, Count Jarnac, the French Minister, and other persons of note.

Lord Aberdeen struck me as one of the most sensible men in England, — grave, thoughtful, prudent, with no pretension or ostentation. He and Everett had a great liking for one another, and he sat to Harding for a portrait, which was in Everett's library till his death. With his youngest son, the well-known Sir Arthur Gordon, recently created Lord Stanmore, I had some pleasant intercourse at a later period.

Pakenham, then British Minister at Washington, had given me a letter to the third Earl of ST. GERMANS, a former Postmaster-General in Peel's Cabinet, previously associated with a mission of mercy to Spain in 1835, when he most successfully negotiated with the two parties to the civil war for an exchange of prisoners, and was the immediate instrument of saving the lives of others at the peril of his own. He was the lineal descendant of that great parliamentary leader, Sir John Eliot, the friend of Hampden, of whom the late John Forster wrote so instructive a biography, by which it seems that Governor Winthrop's reasons for coming to New England were the subject of consideration and correspondence between Eliot and Hampden while Eliot was imprisoned in the Tower.

I remember visiting the Tower in company with Lady St. Germans and her son Granville Eliot (who fell in the Crimean campaign), and we lingered in the room where this great martyr of bold and free speech died. Lady St. Germans was a granddaughter of Lord Cornwallis, and one day when I had been dining with her husband he showed me the sword of Tippoo Saib, which Cornwallis captured in India, — adding pleasantly that he was not able to show me the sword Cornwallis wore at Yorktown, as he unfortunately lost it!

Lord St. Germans was subsequently Lord-Lieutenant of Ireland and Lord Steward of the Queen's household, in which latter capacity he accompanied the Prince of Wales to the United States. Nothing could exceed his repeated kindness to me and mine, and our friendship ended only with his death in 1877. Lady St. Germans, a most amiable and excellent woman, died on the very day (it has been said) on which her son's regiment entered London in triumph on its return from the Crimea, and when a fresh sense of her bereavement was forced upon her already shattered health.

My passing allusion to Sir RICHARD PAKENHAM recalls our intimacy while I was in Congress and he Minister at Washington. He was a frank, hearty, honest Irishman, with no diplomatic reserve or equivoque about him, with no superabundance of accomplishment, but with talent and experience enough to do his work advantageously for England and acceptably for our govcrnment. His predecessor was another bachelor, HENRY STEPHEN Fox (nephew of Charles James Fox), whose eccentricities were the laugh of Washington when I first entered Congress. Rising generally when other people were almost ready to go to bed, when a ceremony or a duty compelled him to an earlier appearance, Fox was like an owl in the daytime. " How strange," said he to Madame Calderon, one morning at a State funeral, — " how strange we look to each other by daylight!" I stood near him at the inauguration of President William Henry Harrison in 1841, and shall never forget how like a figure of fun he looked, with a uniform which he had outgrown, and which he had probably brought from Brazil, his white cassimere trousers barely reaching his ankles, and his *chapeau de bras* tawny with time and use! As Harrison alluded to foreign nations, Fox, as *doyen* of the diplomatic corps, advanced slowly toward him; but before he could get near enough to hear, the President had changed his topic to " our brethren, the red men." The expression, half smile and half chagrin, which came over Fox's face at that moment, as he fell back into the throng, defies description. His debts compelled him to economy, and he rarely gave dinners. A year or two before I knew him, he had invited a large party to his house, — Mr. Clay, Mr. Calhoun, Mr. Webster, and all the giants (for there were giants in those days), — and when they were all assembled, he said, " Gentlemen, now be good enough to put on your hats and follow me." And thus saying, he led the way to a neighboring eating-house! But he was an agreeable and accomplished man, with a noble head and a ready wit; and nobody could have been more agreeable than he was at a little dinner given for the historian Prescott by our friend Calderon de la Barca, the Spanish Minister. His death at Washington from an overdose of opium sufficiently revealed the secret of his oddity,—if, indeed, it had been a secret to any one who saw and knew him.

Pakenham had not a particle of Fox's peculiarity, and rendered himself all the more acceptable by the contrast. It happened that he was in Ireland on leave when I visited Dublin in 1847; and as I could not accept his pressing invitation to go to him in the country, he came to Dublin and spent four or five days with me. We drove to Donnybrook Fair together in a jaunting car, and the next day to Castletown (the princely seat of his cousin, Colonel Connolly), and the day after drove through the Powerscourt demesne in the beautiful county Wicklow. We dined together, too, with Lord Clarendon, then Lord-Lieutenant, at the Vice-regal Lodge in Phœnix Park, and at Sir Philip' Crampton's at Lough Bray. Thus the only regret I had at being unable to visit him was from losing the promised privilege of seeing Miss Edgeworth, the authoress, who was a near neighbor and friend of his. At home or abroad, at Washington or in Dublin, Sir Richard was a delightful companion, and his constant kindness attached me strongly to him.

Nor can I say much less of Sir JOHN CRAMPTON, who succeeded Sir Richard, and who was the son of Sir

Philip, my host at Lough Bray. The latter, by the way, was a great surgeon, and had been medical adviser to all the Lord-Lieutenants for nearly half a century. Among others he had attended the Marquis of Wellesley, and had been intimate with him and our American Mrs. Patterson at the time of their courtship and marriage. I should not venture to put on paper his account of their love passages, which were at once comic and pathetic. Sir Philip looked younger than his son, whose premature white hairs when he came to Washington suggested sixty instead of forty. The frost was only on the outside, however, and he had not a little amiability as well as ability.

After Crampton came Sir HENRY BULWER, afterward Lord Dalling, the very impersonation of diplomacy, — artful, accomplished, capable of intrigue, not afflicted with scruples, though a valetudinarian in all other respects; a man of real talent and of many agreeable qualities, a charming writer and a good speaker, whose compliments at public dinners were always gracefully turned.

After Bulwer came Lord NAPIER, not inferior to Bulwer in the arts of diplomacy, superior to him in the graces, and of a personal figure and address quite fascinating. He was a man of great elegance, and rendered himself exceedingly agreeable in social life. His little speech at the Harvard festival, while I was President of the Alumni, was one of the most felicitous I ever heard. His admiration for Washington Allston's coloring was unbounded. He told me repeatedly that no other living artist of any country could have painted such pictures; and he tried hard to persuade the British Government to purchase one for the National Gallery in London. Lord Napier had himself written a book on modern Italian art, of which I have a copy, though not of his gift, for he said he was ashamed of it, and would not let me see it. He gave me, however, an interesting biography of his ancestor, the great Master of Napier and author of Logarithms, by his cousin the late Mark Napier. Lord Napier was a delightful companion during a summer which I passed with him at the Nahant hotel, where I formed the acquaintance of his lovely wife, — one of the most saintly persons I have ever known, as full of goodness of heart as of grace and sweetness of manner, and whose image will always have a place in my little gallery of cherished memories.

The Napiers were followed by Lord Lyons, an excellent man of business, a bachelor, and wholly wedded to his profession, — a plain, blunt, genial Englishman, with not a little touch of the sailor manner, which he may have caught from the Admiral his father. I had long been out of Congress when he was at Washington, but met him frequently elsewhere, and dined at least once with him there at his own table, when Everett and I went on to present a memorial for peace just before the Civil War. I dined with him afterward in Paris, where he was long Ambassador, and in London, after he had retired from that post. An ancestor of his, Capt. Henry Lyons, of Antigua, married a granddaughter of Governor Winthrop's son Samuel, who was himself Deputy-Governor of Antigua, so that we called ourselves kinsmen.

He was, if I mistake not, a minister of more practical ability than any England had sent to America since Mr. STRATFORD CANNING, the late Lord Stratford de Redcliffe, whom I also knew and with whom I remember dining in 1867. He then had a great desire to talk about his old friend John Quincy Adams, who was our Secretary of State while he was Minister at Washington. A man of grand presence, somewhat stern and stately, he knew how to unbend gracefully, and was long one of the most impressive and interesting figures in the House of Lords. The recent biography of him, by Stanley Lane Poole, does no more than justice to his really great career and character, and, as Dean Stanley truly said in a sermon in Westminster Abbey the day after his funeral: "No one could enter into his presence, either as he sat on what may be called his throne at Constantinople, or during the long years of his dignified retirement, without feeling that they had seen a king of men."

Lord Lyons was succeeded at Washington by Sir FREDERICK BRUCE, an amiable and excellent man, whose diplomatic career was cut short by his much-regretted death in Boston, after a short illness. I had previously known his elder brothers: Lord ELGIN, when Governor-General of Canada, and General ROBERT

BRUCE, when head of the Prince of Wales's household. All three brothers made a very agreeable impression in society, both at home and abroad.

Of English men of letters I have already mentioned Rogers and Wordsworth, Hallam and Milman, but I must not forget Earl STANHOPE, the historian, — Lord Mahon, as he was when I first knew him, — a laborious student and an earnest seeker after truth, whose works will always be consulted for their substantial merits, and as valuable authorities on the subjects to which they relate. My relations with him and his charming wife were particularly pleasant, and I was among the many who mourned the untimely death of his attractive daughter, the late Lady Beauchamp.

At a breakfast at Stanhope's one of the guests was THACKERAY, whom I had known in America, when he was more than once at my house. I always associate him with a visit I paid my dear friend, John Pendleton Kennedy, in Washington, where he was then Secretary of the Navy, and while Washington Irving was my only fellow-guest. One dinner at Kennedy's, with Irving, Thackeray, and Tom Corwin, lingers in my memory. Wit, humor, anecdote, reminiscence, and sparkling merriment abounded to overflowing. Thackeray was approaching his end when I met him at Lord Stanhope's, and ominous shadows were gathering over his brow. He apologized for not calling upon me on account of infirmities, but begged me to come to see him before I left London. I did so, and found him, as he said, "taking his first tea and toast for

many days." His daughter was ministering to him,
and he seemed really ill. His somewhat cynical tem-
perament was not, however, wholly subdued. "Do
you know an American named Allibone?" said he.
" He has sent me a big Dictionary, and wants me to
acknowledge it; but I have not done it, and do not
mean to." I told him I knew Dr. Allibone well, and
valued him highly; that his Dictionary of Authors
was a work of great labor, and as useful in its way
as the *Dictionnaire des Contemporains* of Vapereau; and
that the author was, like Vapereau, one of the most
obliging of men. "I thank you, I thank you," said
he, instantly, "for this explanation. I will write to
him at once, and make amends for my neglect." And
he did write to him in a cordial and complimentary
style, as I subsequently learned from Allibone himself. Thackeray's cynicism was only skin-deep. He
had a large heart below.

I did not meet DICKENS in England, though I had
seen much of him at Washington during his first visit
to America.[1] He then brought me a letter of introduction from Mr. Everett, our Minister to England,
while I was keeping house at Washington with Kennedy.
Kennedy and I called at once and asked him to dine;
but he had made his engagements long before his
arrival at Washington, and was obliged to refuse all
new invitations. He thus refused to dine at the
President's and at Ex-President John Quincy Adams's,
so that we lesser notabilities had no cause to complain.

---

[1] I was in Europe when he came last.

I dined with him at Mayor Seaton's, when Mrs. Madison, Clay, and Webster were among the guests, and afterward took him and Mrs. Dickens to the President's reception, where we revolved around the East Room together, Dickens on one side of me and his wife on the other, and they were the observed of all observers. As we were leaving, the colored drivers on the portico shouted, "Lord Boz's carriage! Lord Boz's carriage!" to our great amusement. John Quincy Adams did not appreciate Dickens. He told me at his own table that, understanding Dickens had letters to him, he had been trying to prepare himself to meet him, and at his daughter-in-law's suggestion had taken up the "Pickwick Papers." "But," said Mr. Adams, "I could not get beyond a few chapters. He has a wonderful faculty of description; but the difficulty is, the things are not worth describing!" And then Mr. Adams launched out into unbounded praise of Fielding, saying that there was no novel like "Tom Jones."

One day — it was Saturday — while Dickens was in Washington, Mr. Adams turned to me and said, "I want you to do me a favor, Mr. Winthrop. You, I know, do not go to dinners, and I do not give them, on Sundays. But Mr. Dickens, having refused my invitation for a dinner next week, has written to say that he wishes the privilege of coming to luncheon with his wife to-morrow at two o'clock. Now, I have no idea of meeting him alone, and I want you and Mr. Saltonstall to come to my aid." So we both went at the hour named. Mrs. Adams had ordered an elaborate lunch, and courses were served as for a dinner. Mr.

and Mrs. Dickens not only came late, but before the meats had been finished, said they must go home and dress for a dinner at the house of a translator in the State Department; and the table of the Ex-President was broken up accordingly! It was a curious instance of the infelicity of the "previous engagements" into which Mr. Dickens had been betrayed by officious friends. He seemed rather to prefer dining with reporters and newspaper men than with persons in official position, and he occasionally exhibited a *brusquerie* and waywardness — perhaps resulting from the flattery he had received at Boston and New York — which led him to put on airs in the company of men entitled to his respect. But his marvellous genius, devoted as it so often was to the cause of philanthropic reform, is enough to secure oblivion for all his infirmities, — more especially when we remember how many of his best characters we should have lost if at one period of his life he had not been fond of low company.

I have already mentioned hearing an eloquent speech from MACAULAY in the House of Commons, and I remember sitting next but one to him at a dinner at Van de Weyer's, the Belgian Minister, and had the full benefit of his wonderful flow of conversation, — I might better say, soliloquy. When I saw him long afterward, he had become a peer and was quite retired from politics. Calling on him at Holly Lodge, Kensington, with a note from Everett, he professed to remember me perfectly, but he was suffering from an asthmatic cough, and had a swollen look which suggested dropsy. His magisterial tone and a certain puffy, panting respiration recalled the accounts of Dr. Johnson. Yet he was kind and cordial, regretting that he was just going out of town, and making me promise that I would come to see him again in the spring, on my return from the Continent. I had a strong presentiment that I should not see him again ; and three or four months afterward, while I was in Paris, the telegraph announced his sudden death. An unfinished letter to Everett was found in the pocket of the coat he had worn last. The two men had many gifts and greatnesses in common. Everett's fame will last longest as a brilliant orator ; Macaulay's as a magnificent writer, almost a second Burke. His Essays will be read even longer than his History, and with less distrust.

BROWNING I have met repeatedly in London and in Rome, dining with him at his own table and at other people's tables. Everywhere he was pleasant and cheery, but he had but little of the poet in social life. He certainly reserved his brilliancy and his profoundness for his verses. His wife I saw only once ; but an hour with her in her own charming apartment left an impression which I can neither forget nor describe.

Of another hour I can recall more. It was with WALTER SAVAGE LANDOR, at his residence in Florence, in February, 1860. A grander old man I have rarely, if ever, seen. He talked much about poetry and the great poets of the world. He ranked them in the following order: Shakspeare, Milton, Homer, Æschylus. Not a word about Dante! Passing to other characters, he placed Washington at the head of all men, and added that next to him, in America, was John Winthrop. Of course he touched my heart, both as to Washington and Winthrop. But I was amazed at his knowing anything about the latter, until he told me that he had held much correspondence with my old friend James Savage, and that incidentally he had become familiar with Mr. Savage's edition of the Governor's journal.

Of JOHN KENYON, also, a name almost forgotten, but worthy of being recalled, I must say a word. Ticknor had given me a letter to him, and nothing could exceed his kindness. His " Rhymed Plea for Tolerance," and his " Day at Tivoli," though praised in " Blackwood " and by Prescott in the " North American Review," will hardly secure him a high place among the poets of his period; but the little volumes were pretty keepsakes, and his friends were always glad to receive and read them. I certainly was. Meantime he was fond of gathering the choicest literary guests around his hospitable board, and his breakfasts and dinners almost rivalled Rogers's. One of them cost me a great disappointment. He had made it especially for me to meet Carlyle; but at the last moment, when it was too late to fill the place, — if such a place could be filled, — illness or caprice prevented Carlyle from keeping his engagement, and so I never saw the old cynic. In a letter to me long ago from the first Lady Ashburton,

5

she said : " Carlyle and Emerson have met, but have discovered that they agree in nothing except in their admiration for each other." I am afraid that if Carlyle and I had met, we should hardly have reached admiration on either side. Yet his " Life of John Sterling," and his " French Revolution," and his " Life and Letters of Cromwell " are admirable in their way. Kenyon had a large fortune, and was munificent in aiding poor authors.

Grote and Bulwer-Lytton I knew but slightly; Darwin and Ruskin not at all, though Canon Farrar was kind enough to take me to the funeral of Darwin in Westminster Abbey. With Lockhart, the younger Lytton, John Forster, and Samuel Warren, Q. C., the genial but now almost forgotten author of " Ten Thousand a Year," I was well acquainted at different periods. Of Froude, Kingsley, Tyndall, and Matthew Arnold, I saw little in their own country, though they all dined with me in America. To Henry Reeve, the accomplished editor of the "Edinburgh Review," and to John Murray, the prince of publishers, I am indebted for many kind attentions. But the English man of letters whom I knew longest and best was RICHARD MONCKTON MILNES, Lord Houghton. I remember breakfasting with him in 1847, when Prince Louis Napoleon, then an exile in London, and Richard Cobden were among the guests. Houghton told me long afterward, that out of the intercourse between Louis Napoleon and Cobden at that breakfast came the commercial treaty between France and England which Cobden negotiated with the Emperor in 1860. I remember dining with Houghton in the last-named year, on the day of the first great Volunteer review by the Queen, when Earl De Grey, then Secretary of War, under whose supervision the review had been arranged and the volunteers organized, was one of the guests. Had he been as successful in arranging the terms of the treaty of Washington with reference to the Alabama Claims, so as to avoid the deplorable misunderstanding which subsequently turned a great act of peace into a fresh cause of contention, he would better have deserved his newer title of Marquis of Ripon. I remember another dinner at Houghton's in 1867, when I sat next to Gladstone, and next but one to John Bright, and greatly enjoyed their brilliant conversation. He gave me on that occasion a photograph of the little church at Austerfield, with the baptismal record of Governor Bradford, and seemed proud of being lord of the manor of that cradle of the Pilgrim Fathers.

Of famous English lawyers I have known few; but I might have added to my reminiscences of Brougham and Lyndhurst that I had been well acquainted with one of their great rivals at the bar and successors on the woolsack, John, Lord CAMPBELL, not the least noticeable incident of whose remarkable career is that he was educated for the Presbyterian ministry. I knew him, however, when he was only Chancellor of the Duchy of Lancaster, with a seat in the House of Commons, and before the publication of any of those biographies of Chief-Justices and Chancellors, with

which his name will always be associated, and which
have been the subject of so much criticism. In later
years, I have repeatedly had·pleasant intercourse with
members of his immediate family.

Distinguished members of the medical profession
often play an important part in London society. I
recall pleasant dinners in 1847, at Sir James Clark's
(then the Queen's leading physician), and at Mr.
(afterward Sir) William Lawrence's, the distinguished
surgeon and man of science. This last was at Ealing
Park, near London, where Mrs. Lawrence's collection
of orchids was one of the marvels of horticulture at
that period.

With Dr. (afterward Sir) HENRY HOLLAND I formed
an agreeable intimacy when he was first in this country,
which lasted until his death in 1873. His wife, the
daughter of the famous wit, Rev. Sydney Smith, added
not a little to the attractions of his well-remembered
home in Brook Street when I first knew it. I recall
there a marble bust of Sydney's elder brother, Robert
Smith, familiarly called Bobus Smith, whom Dr. Holland pronounced " the most accomplished scholar and
the most profound thinker" he had ever known. His
name was then new to me, and, of course, made the
stronger impression. Before my second visit to England, in 1859, Dr. Holland had become a baronet. He
was a great traveller. Though devoted to the practice
of his profession, he found time in his midsummer and
autumn vacations for seeing many lands; and at the
end of his long life he had left hardly any place of

note unvisited. His "Recollections of a Past Life" contain the story of his various journeys and voyages, year after year, with most interesting accounts of places and persons. Hardly any other man of his time could have met and known so many people worth meeting and knowing. Sir Henry gave me an advance copy of this little volume in 1868, before it was enlarged and published, and when he had printed only a few copies for his family and friends. I remember well how much it was enjoyed by Ticknor and Dr. Jacob Bigelow and Oliver Wendell Holmes and others of my friends to whom I loaned it on my return home, — one of whom returned it with a letter saying that before returning it " he had revelled in a second reading of it." Sir Henry had crossed the Atlantic seven times before his death, and had visited successively almost all parts of our land, — " travelling," as he said, " over nearly twenty-three thousand miles of the American continent." I was a fellow-passenger with him in 1869, and found him a brave and delightful companion in storm as well as in sunshine. He spent many days of the last week of this last visit to America under my roof at Brookline, — coming over to me from a briefer visit to our friend the late Charles Francis Adams, at Quincy. He was a fine scholar, and always travelled with a volume or two of the classics in his bag, to occupy and divert his spare moments. As he bade me good-by for the last time, he said quietly that he had left a little " Virgil " on the table in his chamber, which had been one of his pet travelling companions all the world over, for many, many

years, and that he had not room for it in his bag any
longer. I might say of it, as of its owner, "Multum
ille et terris jactatus et alto." It bears the marks of
hard usage, but is not the less interesting on that
account. With his eldest son, the statesman and
cabinet minister, now Lord Knutsford, and his attractive wife, a favorite niece of Lord Macaulay, I have
had some pleasant intercourse in later years.

Of English prime ministers of the last half-century,
Peel, Aberdeen, and Derby I have already mentioned.
With Lords RUSSELL and BEACONSFIELD my acquaintance was but slight. I never heard either of them
make a speech of any importance, but I have enjoyed
several of the latter's witty novels. Lords PALMER-
STON and SALISBURY I knew better, having lunched
with the latter at his famous seat of Hatfield, and
having repeatedly attended the former's Saturday
evening receptions. His cordial, jaunty air was full
of fascination, and I could quite understand the social
as well as political influence exercised by Lady Palmerston and himself. He had the commanding presence
and unfailing tact of Henry Clay, with, of course,
something more of the polish of a trained courtier.
An intense Briton, he cared little for the rights of
other countries so he could uphold or increase the
power and prestige of his own. My interest in
meeting him was enhanced by the recollection that he
was the last male representative of the most distinguished branch of that once numerous family of
Temple, another branch of which was represented in

the last century by my maternal grandfather, Sir John Temple. A niece of the last-named was the grandmother of an eminent Englishman who is not yet prime minister, but who would do honor to that exalted station, — the present Marquis of DUFFERIN, who has gone through a succession of great offices and made a distinguished mark in each one of them. Wherever and whenever England has looked for a man to meet a sudden exigency, — whether as Viceroy of India or ambassador at different courts, — she has called upon him, and never called in vain. As a speaker and writer, he has not a few of the charms of his great-grandfather, Richard Brinsley Sheridan. His " Letters from High Latitudes" was one of the wittiest books of its day; and his social attractions have rendered him a delightful companion wherever he has been known on either continent. I recall with pleasure a visit of several days which he and Lady Dufferin paid me at Brookline when he was Governor-General of Canada, and I have often enjoyed his society in London.

Of the new prime minister, Lord ROSEBERY, too, I have seen something on both sides of the ocean, but it was at an early period of his life when so distinguished a future could hardly have been confidently predicted for him. His illustrious predecessor, GLADSTONE, I have been privileged to meet often, either at his own table or at the tables of others. I doubt if any man I ever met has impressed me more by the wealth of his accomplishments, by the charms of his conversation, and by a certain transparency of character, than

Gladstone. Yet it is often complained that no one can quite see through him; and it must be confessed that the clearness of his ideas is sometimes obscured by the exuberance of his vocabulary.

The most interesting speech I ever heard him make was at an evening meeting of the Society of Antiquaries. Lord Stanhope (then President of that Society) had given a little dinner at which Gladstone, the Duke of Argyll, Dr. Schliemann the explorer, Longfellow, and I were among the guests. After our adjournment to Burlington House, Schliemann proceeded to give a very graphic account of his then recent discoveries, illustrating them with maps prepared for the occasion. The subject was at once familiar and fascinating to Gladstone, who rose after Schliemann had finished and spoke for nearly an hour, delighting all who listened to him. His has indeed been a wonderful career; but while no one can have beheld without a feeling of admiration the physical and intellectual vigor which has enabled him till now to bear the brunt of parliamentary warfare, some of us, on the other hand, may be inclined to doubt whether his fame would not have been as great, or greater, if he had retired earlier from politics, and devoted the remainder of his life to literature.

In running my eye over these desultory but by no means exhaustive reminiscences, I find myself continually reminded of other valued friends of different periods, — such, for instance, as Dr. VAUGHAN, long Master of the Temple and now Dean of Llandaff, and good Dean Howson of Chester, and the lamented Principal Tulloch of St. Andrews, — while I am conscious that still other names, to which I should like to have made passing allusion, will not occur to me until too late. I feel, however, that it is only grateful to devote a line to that kindest of hosts, Thomas Baring, M. P. (Tom Baring, as he was so generally called), long senior partner of the great house of that name, who might have been Chancellor of the Exchequer if he had chosen. Nor should I forget that accomplished scholar, the most amiable and unpretending of men, the seventh Duke of Devonshire, under whose auspices as Chancellor of the University of Cambridge I received the degree of Doctor of Laws in 1874, in company with Sir Bartle Frere, Lord Chief Justice Cockburn, and Lord Wolseley. His eldest son, the present Duke, a prime minister of the future, I also knew under his former title of Hartington, and have since had occasion to realize how much ability and patriotic purpose lie concealed under his apathetic manner and hesitating delivery. A younger brother of the last-named, Lord Frederick Cavendish, I knew much better, and there still lingers in my ears the cry of the newsboys under my window in London, in 1882, announcing his shameful murder by Irish assassins, — the most brutal political crime of the nineteenth century, and the untimely ending of a career of promise.

If I have said nothing of three other English statesmen of whom I have seen something at different times, — two of them the foremost debaters of their day in the Commons (Sir WILLIAM HARCOURT and Mr. CHAMBERLAIN), the other a useful member of both houses of Parliament in succession, and justly esteemed for his scientific attainments and rare social gifts (Lord PLAYFAIR), — it is because they have all three had the good taste to marry Massachusetts wives, and their characters and careers are as familiar in this country as in their own.

I was first presented at Court in 1847. Mr. Bancroft, our Minister, was unfortunately taken ill a few days before the Drawing-Room, and I accompanied Mr. Brodhead and Mr. Moran, his secretaries, having been admitted by Lord Palmerston to the diplomatic circle, where VAN DE WEYER, the Belgian Minister, took me kindly in charge. After making my bow, I was thus privileged to remain in the Court circle, and witness the presentations from beginning to end. The Queen was then in the full enjoyment of youth and health, and was surrounded by all the beauty of her Court, — the Duchess of Sutherland, the Marchioness of Douro, and Lady Jocelyn among the most conspicuous. Prince Albert was at her side, and the young Grand Duke Constantine of Russia near him; while the old Duke of Wellington was not far off. It was a splendid scene. Soon afterward I was at a ball at Buckingham Palace; and before leaving London, I attended the Birthday Drawing-Room, and was again witness to the grace and dignity of the Queen's manner. But the best opportunity I had of seeing and hearing her was in the House of Lords, when she prorogued Parliament in person. Nothing could have been more brilliant than that occasion, — the peers in their robes, the peeresses in all their jewels, floor and galleries crowded with all the distinction and beauty of the realm, the Queen herself in her state attire, with a crown upon her head. But more impressive than anything else was the distinct articulation and exquisite voice with which she read her speech. Fanny Kemble in Portia was not more effective. The whole scene was dramatic, and no part could have been better played than that of her Majesty; while the solemnity and sincerity of her tone sufficiently evinced that she was not playing a part at all, but discharging a duty with simple, unconscious earnestness.

Thirteen years afterward I was at Court again, with our Minister, Mr. Dallas. The Queen and the Prince Consort had lost the freshness of youth, and gave plain indication that the cares of royalty had not weighed upon them lightly.

Seven years later still, I accompanied Mr. Adams on his last attendance at a Drawing-Room. But there was no Queen, and no Prince Consort. The good and wise Prince had been dead for five or six years, and her Majesty had not emerged from her long mourning for him. Two of her daughters, with the Prince of Wales, took her place. The ceremony was cold and brief, and the Court very thinly attended. A greater contrast to the Drawing-Room of 1847 could not have been imagined. My own old Court dress, reappearing at the end of twenty years, seemed to me the only reminder of my first presentation. But I was glad to have accompanied Mr. Adams, and to have witnessed the respect with which he was then regarded.

Of the PRINCE OF WALES I saw not a little when he was in Boston, having been on the committee for his reception. Longfellow and I were of the committee of three, with Commodore Hudson, for conducting him to the ball, and he was specially committed to my charge. The pains he took the next morning, in the Library at Cambridge, in returning a little pencil which he had borrowed of me for writing down his partners for the dance, and which I had told him was not worth return-ing, impressed me with an idea of his thoughtfulness; and the interest he manifested in the autographs of Washington and Franklin (of which I gave him speci-mens, at his own suggestion, from my own family papers) evinced both intelligence and tact.

It happened that Longfellow and I were standing together on the lawn at a garden-party at Holland House in 1867, when the Prince, who was among the guests, came up and greeted us cordially. After a little talk about Boston and his visit to the United States, he asked us to go with him and let him recall us to the Comte de Paris. Nothing could have been kinder or more graceful than his manner. A few days later, he sent us a special invitation to call on him at Marlbo-rough House, where we spent half an hour with him. On taking leave, he excused himself for not offering us some more formal hospitality on account of the Princess's recent confinement, and said to me in parting, " Re-

member me to all my Boston friends." Soon afterward I met him at a ball at Earl Spencer's, when he
crossed the room to shake hands with me, and presented
me to the French Ambassador, Prince La Tour d'Au-
vergne. I was most agreeably disappointed in his whole
air and aspect, and entirely discredited the malicious
gossip which prevailed about him at that time.

Seven years later, in 1874, at a state concert in
Buckingham Palace, I was gratified to find that he still
remembered me, and he took pains to present both my
wife and myself to the Princess. At a garden-party at
Lambeth Palace not long after, he again honored me
with some little conversation; and he has left on my
mind the impression of exceeding courtesy, with that
royal gift, a good memory for faces.

I was not less favorably impressed with Prince
ARTHUR, whom I met at the funeral of George Peabody
at Danvers, and who was among the hearers of my
eulogy on that occasion. There was a singular grace
and graciousness about him, and of course I could not
but feel gratified and flattered by his asking me to send
him (as I did) two copies of my eulogy, — "one for
himself, and the other," as he said, "for his mother."
Long afterward, her Majesty did me the great honor to
send me a copy of "Our Life in the Highlands" with
her autograph; but I attributed this favor not to any
merit of my own, but to my having become known to
her as a friend of Dean Stanley and as associated by
Mr. Peabody in some of his public benefactions.

Crossing the Channel in June, 1847, I spent hardly more than a fortnight at that time in Paris, and saw but few persons. Prescott had given me a letter to Comte ADOLPHE DE CIRCOURT, who from that time until his death in 1879 was one of my most valued friends and correspondents. Speaking and writing the English language perfectly, he always seemed to me a man of the most universal knowledge and accomplishment I have ever known. He had reviewed Prescott's " Ferdinand and Isabella" in the Bibliothèque Universelle de Genève, six or seven years before I knew him, and had greatly gratified Prescott and his friends. He was soon to be intrusted with an important mission to Berlin, and to win from Lamartine a tribute such as hardly any other man of his time and country has ever received. " This person," says Lamartine, " little known as yet out of the aristocratic world, a man of literature and learning, is M. de Circourt. He had been employed in diplomacy under the Restoration. The revolution of July had thrown him into retirement and opposition, — being more inclined to legitimacy than to democracy. He had profited by these years of seclusion to devote himself to studies which would have absorbed many men's lives, but which were only the diversions of his own. Languages, races, geography, history, philosophy, travels, constitutions, religions of people from the infancy of the world down to our own day, from Thibet even to the Alps, — he had incorporated them all into his mind; had reflected upon them all, had retained them all. One might question him on the universality of facts and ideas which make up the world, without his being obliged, in order to answer, to consult other volumes than his own memory, — an immense extent and surface and depth of notions, of which no one ever knew the bottom or the limits; a living world-chart of human knowledge. . . . M. de Circourt had married a young Russian girl, of an aristocratic family and of a European spirit. Through her he had relations to all that was eminent in the literary or court circles of Germany and of the North."

De Candolles, the great botanist, bears similar testimony to the marvellous acquirements and accomplishments of M. de Circourt, and gives more than one most striking anecdote of the young Russian girl, Anastasia de Klustein, who, when I was in Paris, had been the Comtesse de Circourt for many years. She was in some respects more remarkable even than her husband, with a vivacity, a *bel esprit*, and a charm of manner altogether her own. Her command of languages seemed almost miraculous. I have been at her salon of a morning or an evening, and heard her converse freely in English, French, Italian, German, and I think Spanish also, besides Russian, her native tongue. She would toss off her questions or answers in either language indifferently, according to the guests who surrounded her, and seemed equally at home in all. The most distinguished men and women of all parties united in admiring and paying homage to her. De Tocqueville and Lamartine and Cavour and Mignet, as well as De Candolles, bore common testimony to her attractions.

I saw Madame de Circourt again in 1859 or 1860, having had more than one charming letter from her in the interval. A few years previously she had been terribly burned, and was now an invalid and a great sufferer; but her physicians permitted her to receive a few friends twice a week, in the morning or evening. Lying on a little sofa, with an anodyne at her side which she occasionally sipped to alleviate anguish, her conversation was as bright and sparkling as it had been thirteen years before, and her repartees in every tongue had lost nothing of their point and pungency. A more heroic endurance of suffering I have never imagined. But a few years more brought it to an end; and her husband long lived alone in his little villa at La Celle St. Cloud, the neighborhood of which during the war with Prussia became the scene of conflict, and its surroundings were greatly changed by the cannon of contending forts and armies. The desolation of his home and the disasters of his country alike bore heavily upon him.

Circourt was never elected to the French Academy. His writings, voluminous as they were in amount, have never taken the form of a volume. Essays and reviews, contributed to periodical journals and never collected, occupied his life. Not a few of them have related to America or Americans. Prescott's "Ferdinand and Isabella," Bancroft's "History of the United States," Kirke's "Charles the Bold," Parkman's "Jesuits in Canada," Motley's "Dutch Republic" too, if I mistake not, Ticknor's "Life of Prescott," and my own "Life and Letters of John Winthrop," have been the subject of elaborate treatment at his hands. Had he devoted himself to a single work, he could not have failed to achieve a fame which these desultory labors have not won, though, after all, perhaps these have been more useful to his fellow-men.

Circourt introduced me to MIGNET, the historian, Perpetual Secretary of the Institute of Moral and Political Sciences. With him I attended an Annual Séance of the Institute, and heard Mignet deliver his commemorative discourse on Ancillon, the eminent Prussian statesman and philosopher. The scene was very striking. The little hall of the Institute was crowded; and a guard of soldiers with muskets not only kept the doors, but were in the very aisles. Some thirty of the most noted literary men of France were in their seats as members, the officers of the Institute wearing green embroidered uniforms, with swords and *chapeaux*. Mignet, in uniform as Secretary, took his seat at the desk in front of the President, and delivered, or rather read, his discourse *ex cathedrâ*. His reading, however, with occasional gestures, was exquisite. A very handsome man, — " le beau Mignet," as he was justly called, — his voice was charming; and Everett himself could not have given more effect to the performance. He was then in the freshness of his manhood. I heard him again in 1860, at the same place, on a similar occasion, and with the same surroundings, deliver, or read, his discourse on Count Portalis. Thirteen years had left little mark on either figure or voice, and I had a renewed impression of the exceeding beauty and grace of his manner. Disliking the Empire and the Emperor, he omitted no opportu-

nity darkly to intimate his dislike, and to make prominent whatever in the career of Portalis had been
hostile to the Imperial policy. The occasion was thus
made a little exciting, and there were rumors afterward that *a caution*, if nothing more, would be issued by
the Imperial Police against such utterances.

I saw Mignet repeatedly at his own house and at my
hotel, and was deeply impressed with the brilliancy of
his conversation. In talking with him about Dupan-
loup, then Bishop of Orleans, whose speeches and
letters I had read with admiration, he said, "Have
you read his Éloge on General La Moricière? There
is nothing finer since Bossuet." I had an opportunity
of reading it shortly afterward, and found it as eloquent as Mignet had described.

I saw him again in 1867, when he had been very ill,
and exhibited the marks of increasing infirmities. He
was obliged to give up his Annual Discourse, or I
should have heard him a third time. He sent me
copies of his Éloges on De Tocqueville and Macaulay,
and gave me his two volumes of Discourses, including
an elaborate and admirable "Notice of Franklin."

I saw a good deal of him again in 1874 and 1875,
dining with him and Barthélemy St. Hilaire in the
latter year at Thiers's table; and on my last visit to
Paris, in 1882, I found him genial and cordial as ever,
engaged in historical composition at the great age of
eighty-six.

Besides the two *séances* of the Institute which I have
mentioned, I was fortunate in being present at two

others, — one in 1874, when De Loménie's description
of Mirabeau was very dramatic; the other in 1882,
when, by the kindness of Barthélemy St. Hilaire, I
assisted at the memorable reception of Cherbuliez by
Ernest Renan and heard eloquent addresses from
both.

I heard GUIZOT make an eloquent speech from the
Tribune of the Chamber of Deputies in 1847, but did
not make his acquaintance until many years later,
when we met repeatedly. Calling upon him at the
close of 1859, he said, —

" Have you anything new this morning ? "

" Nothing," I replied, " but the sudden death of
Macaulay, as announced by telegraph from London."

" Macaulay dead ! " he exclaimed.   " He was my
best friend in England ; " and he could hardly conceal
or contain his emotion.

Guizot spoke English perfectly, but THIERS not a
word. If he could speak a word, he never would. I
had taken a letter and parcel for him from London to
Paris from William Bingham Baring, afterward second
Lord Ashburton, who made me promise to leave my
own card with them. The card of Thiers was immediately returned ; and soon afterward Mr. Martin, then
our Chargé d'Affaires, accompanied me to a reception
at his house in Place St. George, subsequently destroyed
by the Communists. Thiers was very cordial ; but
finding that my French would hardly hold out for
a political discussion, he passed me on politely to
his wife, who spoke English fluently. I was again at

his house in 1867, and while waiting for him to come in, I had a good chance to observe the beauty of his pictures and objects of art, so many of which the Communists have destroyed or ruined. I heard him in the Chamber, too, more than once, in reply to Rouher, and during some of the most exciting debates on the Roman question and other agitating subjects. I shall never forget his exclamation, twice repeated with the most passionate emphasis: " Soyons Français! Soyons Français! " The pitch of enthusiasm to which the Chamber rose at that moment exceeded anything I had ever witnessed in a so-called deliberative body. But the Chamber was always in a state of excitement, and often of confusion, during the debates in those last years of the Empire; and a stranger would have thought that they might pass from words to blows at any moment. Yet Rouher maintained a comparative tranquillity and dignity of manner, and had a certain *pose*, when he ascended the tribune, which recalled Webster's manner to me. Thiers more than once reminded me of John Quincy Adams in some of his most violent moods during the antislavery debates in Congress. I was greatly impressed by the fire of French eloquence at that time. When Thiers sent me a copy of his most elaborate speech, I little imagined how soon he would be ruling the destinies of a French republic; but quite as little had I imagined, in 1847, how soon Louis Philippe would be dethroned, and be succeeded, after a brief republican interregnum, by an Emperor.

I was presented to Louis Philippe by Mr. Martin, our Chargé d'Affaires (after Mr. King of Alabama had left Paris, and before Mr. Rush had arrived), at the Palace of Neuilly. It was a quiet evening reception, and I was invited, out of regular course, as a member of Congress. The British Ambassador (Lord Normanby) and Leverrier, then in the first flush of his celebrity as the discoverer of the new planet, were almost the only visitors besides myself and Mr. Martin. There were two or three aides-de-camp in uniform; but the King was in plain clothes, and the Queen and Madame Adelaide and the Duchess of Orleans were sitting at a little table, sipping their tea and then turning to their embroidery. Nothing could have been more simple and unaffected than the manners of them all. The Duchess of Orleans, with whom I conversed most, was particularly graceful and gracious, and gave me an impression of goodness and loveliness which was fully confirmed by her Life and Letters, as published after her death. Her son, the Comte de Paris, was a little boy then, and had doubtless gone to bed; but I have known him since in London and in Boston, and he has been good enough to send me his volume on the Trades-Unions of England, and his valuable History of our Civil War. He has always impressed me as the worthy son of so excellent a mother. Louis Philippe himself was cordial and chatty, asking after Americans whom he had known when in the United States as an exile. " Did you know Tim Pickering ? " said he, and then went on to say more than I can remember of him and others of our old-time statesmen. He followed me almost to the door of the room, in the easiest way, when I took my leave, and told me emphatically that I must come and see him again. Mr. Martin said this was a royal command, and must be obeyed; and so the next week I went again, — this time in plain clothes, for I was in uniform before. Another conversation with the Duchess of Orleans renewed my impression of the sweetness and sincerity of her manner and character; and the King was as jaunty and as cordial as before. In seven or eight months more, he and his family were banished from France, and the palace in which I had seen them was sacked and burned.

My pleasant associations with the royal family of Orleans were revived and intensified thirty-five years later, in September, 1882, by being privileged, through the kind offices of M. Laugel, to lunch with that distinguished soldier and historical writer, the Duc d'Aumale, at his well-known Château of Chantilly, where he was good enough to show me in person many of the priceless works of art which it contains.

Of LAMARTINE, whose three months of power succeeded the downfall of the Orleans dynasty, and whose eloquence arrested the madness of the Red Republicans of that period, I saw nothing in 1847. But having alluded to him, in July, 1848, in my oration on laying the corner-stone of the monument to Washington, as Speaker of the House of Representatives of the United States, I received from him a letter of acknowledgment which was very characteristic, and is worthy of a place here : —

MONSIEUR, — Les *cordes magiques* m'ont apporté le magnifique fragment de votre discours, où mon nom bien indigne d'un pareil honneur est associé par vous à la mémoire de Washington. Cette allusion m'a été d'autant plus douce, en ce moment, que je me trouve dans ma patrie sous la poids d'une immense dépression, conséquent d'une immense erreur sur les motifs de ma conduite politique, après que j'ai été assez heureux pour contribuer à remettre cette patrie sauvée dans les mains de l'Assemblée Nationale. J'ai trop lu et trop écrit l'histoire pour m'étonner d'un mal entendu d'opinion, ni même pour m'affliger d'une persécution morale. Je sais combien l'humanité est susceptible d'erreur, et quelquefois même avide d'ingratitude. Néanmoins je vous remercie d'avoir envoyé avec votre discours ici un certain remords à quelques-uns de mes compatriotes. La justice qui vient de loin est celle qui arrive la première, parce que elle est ordinairement la plus impartiale. Il y a cependant une bien grande partialité dans vos paroles sur moi ; mais c'est la partialité de la bienveillance qui unit entre eux à travers l'océan les républicains du même cœur. C'est de cette partialité, Monsieur, que je devois me plaindre, car elle m'écrase en me louant. Je n'en ai pas la force. Je saisis au contraire avec empressement ce prétexte pour vous addresser non seulement ma reconnaissance, mais mon admiration desintéressée pour votre discours, qui sera aussi un monument à l'Amérique, à la vraie liberté, et à Washington.

Recevez, Monsieur, mes respectueux et affectueux compliments,

LAMARTINE,
Représentant du Peuple.

À l'honorable ROBERT WINTHROP,
Président de la Chambre de Représentants.

On one of my next visits to Paris, in 1859 or 1860, I eagerly complied with the invitation of Lamartine, through a friend, and passed an evening at his house. There was something more than usually interesting in his appearance, and his voice was exceedingly rich. As he walked the room, conversing, or rather soliloquizing, in the most emphatic and almost impassioned manner, his vibratory tones combined with his tall figure, and a somewhat dictatorial manner, to remind me of some scenes between Mr. Clay and myself at Washington. Unfortunately, he either could not or would not speak a word of English, albeit his wife was an Englishwoman. His remarks in regard to the United States, and particularly on the subject of slavery, were by no means agreeable to me, and I was roused to muster up all my resources in reply. I think I can safely say that I talked more bad French that night to the poet-statesman of France than I had ever done before, or than I have ever done since, to any one. The failure of his subscription-list in America had greatly disappointed him; and his own downfall, after so brief a term of authority, had served to sour him generally. Yet I have found much to admire in Lamartine's genius and heroism, and I was charmed with some parts of his conversation that evening. We parted most amicably, and he soon afterward called upon me at my hotel; but I was out, and saw him no more.

I have already mentioned having met NAPOLEON III. in London in 1847. I breakfasted with him at

Monckton Milnes's, lunched with him at Miss Burdett-Coutts's, dined with him at Joshua Bates's, and we exchanged cards. There was an air of modest reticency about him then, which was quite attractive. At Miss Burdett-Coutts's he was accompanied by Doctor Conneau, and by the dog which had been a party to his escape from the prison at Ham. On my return to London in 1859, at a matinée at Miss Burdett-Coutts's, the first person I was presented to at the head of the stairs, on entering, was the Comte de Paris, then an exile ; while, on crossing the Channel again, I found Louis Napoleon, the exile of 1847, on the throne! No Court receptions were then being held, but at the suggestion of a former French Minister to the United States, who had known me as Speaker and Senator, I wrote a note to Mocquard, the private secretary of the Emperor, expressing a disposition to wait upon his Majesty. Meantime, however, our Secretary of Legation, Mr. Calhoun (then acting as Chargé d'Affaires), had sent in my name ; but delays, resulting from the state of public affairs, prevented any appointment for an audience reaching me until I had gone a day's journey on my way to Italy.

In 1868, I was more fortunate, and through the kindness of General Dix — at that time our Minister to France — had the pleasure of accompanying him to one of the *petits lundis* of the Empress. Beautiful she certainly was that evening, and singularly graceful and winning. In alluding to my country and country- . men, she gave me a chance to name Washington Irving, who had often told me of his intimacy in her

family, and that he had had the Empress as a child on
his knee. I did not, of course, go into such particu-
lars; but she instantly caught at his name, saying,
"And did you know Washington Irving? And was
he a friend of yours? He was a delightful person and
a delightful writer!" On the Emperor saying to me
rather significantly, "You have been in Europe before,
M. Winthrop," I said that I could not forget having
met his Majesty at Mr. Bates's in London, twenty
years before. "Oh, yes! and what a good man Mr.
Bates was!" said he. "And what a good American!"
he immediately added. Thus I had elicited imperial
compliments for two of my countrymen, and was
content.

The scene was a magnificent one, without the pomp
and ceremony of a grand reception, but also without
its crowd and confusion. After the first formal entrée,
the Emperor and Empress moved freely about among
their guests, and every one was put at his ease. The
music, the toilettes, the flowers, the supper, were all
exquisite; but I had witnessed a still more magnificent pageant of the Empire a few months before, when
I was present at the opening of the Chambers at the
beginning of the New Year. That was a state ceremony, like the one I had witnessed in London in 1847,
and I hardly know which was the more imposing, —
the opening of the French Chambers by the Emperor,
or the prorogation of Parliament by the Queen. The
Emperor at sixty could hardly be expected to deliver
his speech as gracefully as the Queen at twenty-five,
but he pronounced it distinctly and bore himself with

great propriety and dignity. All the high officers of the court and the army were present, with the Empress and her ladies of honor, and the Prince Imperial and all the imperial family, making a superb spectacle. How little did those who witnessed it, or those who participated in it, dream of the reverses which France and its imperial rulers were so soon to undergo! I have always thought it noble of Napoleon III. to avow his personal responsibility for the surrender at Sedan, nor can I doubt that the reasons he assigned for order-ing the surrender were sufficient; but the war with Prussia was a terrible mistake, if it could have been avoided. Yet if there had been no Sedan, the war might have been esteemed wise, or certainly would have been called so.

Of his successors at the helm of France (besides Thiers, whom I have already mentioned) I have been received at the Élysée by both Presidents MACMAHON and GRÉVY, while I had the good fortune to meet GAMBETTA after his fall from power. Marshal Macmahon impressed me as a courteous, high-minded soldier; Grévy as rather a homespun person with but little conversation; Gam-betta I found much more of a gentleman than I expected, with a wonderful voice, a striking carriage, and an air of conscious strength.

But for the risk of becoming tedious, I might easily mention other Parisian celebrities, of less historical importance, with whom at different periods I have been brought into contact, and some of whom I met at the well-known receptions of Madame MOHL. I content

myself, however, with briefly alluding to several opportunities I enjoyed of appreciating the charm of French
rural life. I had long been no stranger to English
country-houses; but it was not until 1882 that I had
an opportunity of comparing them with French ones,
having in that year passed a few pleasant days with
the Marquis de ROCHAMBEAU at his ancestral château
near Vendôme, where I occupied the tapestried bed-
room of the Maréchal de Rochambeau of Revolutionary
memory, which contained a portrait of Washington,
given by himself. My agreeable acquaintance with
the present Marquis, dated from the previous year,
when he had come to America as an invited guest at
the ceremonies attending the centennial anniversary
of the surrender at Yorktown, on which occasion I had
delivered a commemorative address by appointment
of Congress. The official deputation from France, by
the way, included General BOULANGER, whose conversation did not then suggest to me or others that he
was a man of much capacity, but whose subsequent
meteoric career and tragic end are too familiar to
require comment.

A few weeks later, I had another pleasant visit,
this time in Normandy, at the country-seat of the
retired ambassador DE CORCELLE, a man full of interesting reminiscence, his wife the granddaughter of
Lafayette, a fine portrait of whom, by Ary Scheffer,
was one of the principal ornaments of the house. The
neighboring country was beautiful; and among the
places I was taken to was Bois Roussel, the seat or
De Corcelle's nephew, Count Roederer, a great French

agriculturist and breeder of race-horses. Another original portrait of Lafayette, together with much of his library, I saw while lunching at his former country-house, the Château de la Grange, then occupied by the venerable Count de LASTEYRIE, who with other members of his family received me very kindly. Madame de Lasteyrie seemed to me quite the most attractive old French lady I had met.

Of Continental celebrities, other than French ones, I have known comparatively few. It so happens that my visits to Berlin have been to enable some member of my family to consult an oculist, at times when the Court was absent, and I have thus never met Bismarck. I had a letter to Humboldt, but he died before I could deliver it; though I had previously received a kind note from him. Some one had sent him a copy of my lecture on "Archimedes and Franklin," on which he had made some comments in a letter to Varnhagen von Ense, which has since been published. I thus had to content myself with visiting his apartment, from which I brought back to Louis Agassiz one of the palms borne by students at his funeral. On the bed on which he died, were some reproductions of Hildebrand's well-known water-color of Humboldt in his library, one of which I had framed as a souvenir.

In Vienna, I have been more fortunate, though when I first went there, in 1859, the great men of the empire were mostly dead, Metternich, for instance, having died in the preceding June. I have, however, known at different times three Austrian Prime Ministers, von RECHBERG, von BEUST, and von BUOL-SCHAUENSTEIN, the last-named a very attractive and interesting person. At a banquet in Vienna in honor of the hundredth anniversary of Schiller's birthday, I met Count THUN and other high officials, to say nothing of some poets and savants whose names I should now have some difficulty in recalling; and at Dr. JÄGER's I met Prince SCHWARZENBERG, though the doctor himself, who had been the physician and friend of Metternich, was the more entertaining person of the two. Nor should I forget that I was invited by the aged Prince ESTERHAZY to his splendid palace, when he talked much of Washington Irving and of Edward Everett, both of whom he had known when Ambassador in London.

My old friend, Senator Seward, was with me during part of my visit to Vienna in the autumn of 1859, and our Minister, Mr. Glancy Jones, obtained for us a private audience of the Emperor, a rare favor at that time. It was stipulated that the conversation should be in German or French, and of course we chose French as the least unfamiliar tongue of the two. Seward, however, with commendable precaution, resolved to study his phrases in advance, and prepared for the occasion a little opening speech, concerning the accuracy of which he consulted my daughter the evening before; and she, fresh from her Ollendorff, revised it for him, greatly to our amusement.

At noon the next day, in evening dress, we drove together to the palace in Mr. Jones's carriage, though neither he nor his secretary was permitted to accompany us. We were ushered to a large ante-chamber in which some of the Hungarian Guard were on duty, one of them standing at the door of the next room with a drawn sword. Presently an aide-de-camp came from it, and took back our names. In a few moments he re-appeared and conducted us to the imperial presence. FRANCIS JOSEPH was in a room of moderate size, in the corner of which was a working-desk with a single chair, from which he rose to receive us. It was evident that no one was to sit there in his presence, as there were no other chairs. The aide-de-camp disappeared; and Seward launched out at once into his little speech, but bungled and broke down in the middle of it. By way of rallying his resources, it occurred to him to offer congratulation on the recent ratification of the treaty of peace with France, and I thought the Emperor seemed to wince at such a reminder of his reverses in Lombardy. I came to the rescue with a word or two about Maria Theresa and some other of the historic glories of Austria. The Emperor then asked a few simple questions about our country and ourselves, and soon signified by a bow that our audience was at an end. He was in un-dress uniform, perfectly natural and unaffected, and I was agreeably disappointed by his apparent intelligence and energy.

I saw him again, reviewing a noble body of cavalry; and surrounded by a brilliant staff in every variety of superb costume. I saw him still again at a concert given in honor of the Schiller Anniversary, in one of the halls of the palace. It was a magnificent entertain-ment, — the Ninth Symphony of Beethoven, with Schiller's Song of Joy, performed by a select orchestra of one hundred, with the aid of the soloists and chorus of the Imperial Opera troupe. The symphony was preceded by the recitation of some of Schiller's most celebrated odes by the great actors of Germany. I had Lord Lytton's admirable version of the odes in my hand, and was thus enabled to appreciate them the better. The Empress sat with her husband in a low gallery at our side, and fulfilled all our expectations by her exceeding grace and beauty.

I have never visited Russia, but I have seen a good deal of Russian diplomates in different parts of the world, and I was intimate with ALEXANDER DE BODISCO, who was for nearly twenty years Minister at Washington, and did so much to create a friendly feeling between the two countries. He delighted in bringing together at his sumptuous table leading men of all parties and sections, and did what he could (aided by his handsome American wife) to soften the asperities and animosities of political controversy.

Bodisco was a character in his way, with a great love of dress, and when he gave a grand ball sometimes wore in succession two showy uniforms in the course of the same evening. Washington was then a comparatively small place, but questions connected with official precedence were as troublesome as they often have been since. Ex-President John Quincy Adams, Senator Benton, and others of the old school, were wont strenuously to contend that the Speaker of the House, as third officer of the nation, should outrank both the Chief-Justice and the Secretary of State. Accordingly, Bodisco, at an entertainment given by him in honor of the marriage of a favorite niece, assigned to me (as Speaker) the duty of leading the way to supper. This proceeding manifestly annoyed James Buchanan, then Secretary of State and afterward President, who was also one of the guests, and whom Bodisco vainly attempted to appease by handing him a knife and requesting him to take the initiative in cutting the bride-cake!

Some three and twenty years later I had the honor of presiding at a banquet given to a younger brother of the present Czar, the Grand Duke ALEXIS, who impressed me as a man of intelligence and accomplishment, with a singularly genial and attractive address. I met him afterward in London, and was reminded that, nearly thirty years before, I had been a privileged spectator of a review of the Household troops by his uncle, the Grand Duke Constantine, who was accompanied on horseback by Prince Albert, the great Duke of Wellington, and a numerous staff, while the royal children were to be seen watching the parade from a window in the Horse Guards.

I was first presented to PIUS IX. in 1860. The late Bishop Fitzpatrick, of Boston, had given me a friendly and flattering letter to Cardinal Antonelli, and I was granted a private audience. The American Minister, Mr. Stockton, accompanied me; and we were ushered into the Pope's private room, where he was sitting in his white flannel or merino robe, with a beautiful

crucifix and a jewelled snuff-box on the table at his
side.

Immediately on our entrance, his Holiness said
to me in French, "Vous avez été Président de la
Chambre et Sénateur?" and on my replying affir-
matively, he continued, "Asseyez-vous, Monsieur," and
then launched out into a most excited discourse on the
then threatened removal of the French troops from
Rome. He spoke altogether in French, and talked
freely and fluently on public affairs on both sides of
the ocean. In the course of his remarks upon America
as "a great country, of great destinies, and enjoying
a great liberty," I reminded him that he was the first
and only Pontiff who had ever crossed the ocean.
He said it was true that as a young priest he had
been in Chili, and no other Pope had gone so far; but
he did not know what might happen hereafter. "We
are in the midst of great events, great changes. I rest
tranquil," said he, "amid them all, trusting in God.
I have no ambition of earthly sovereignty, and am
content to part with temporal power whenever God
so wills it. But I do not wish, nor is it my duty, to
accept the decrees of mortal kings or emperors as
indications or instruments of God's will."

He more than intimated his belief that the Emperor
of the French had already, at that very moment, given
orders to Marshal Vaillant to withdraw his troops from
Italy. Mr. Stockton suggested that it was probably
only from the north of Italy. The Pope replied that
he supposed the troops might not be removed quite so
summarily from Rome; the Emperor ought certainly

to give more than two hours' notice, — a week or two was the least that should be given. But he was not altogether at the mercy of foreign troops, and he trusted all would be safe whether they went or stayed. And then he made an eloquent and impassioned allusion to the exquisite fresco of Heliodorus by Raphael, and to the intervention of a Divine Protector portrayed in that grand picture. Nothing could have been more impressive than this part of his conversation, and I regret that I cannot recall more of it. He spoke with great approbation of a recent speech or letter of the late Archbishop Hughes, and of some manifestation which he himself had just received from Buffalo. But he seemed not to know exactly where Buffalo was, until I referred to it as being not far from the great Falls of Niagara. He spoke most gratefully of the sympathy which had been manifested for Rome, not merely by Catholics, but by Protestants throughout the world, alluding particularly — if I mistake not — to some recent act of the Grand Duchess of Mecklenburg, among others.

Rome was at that time in a state of great agitation. There were daily rumors that the French garrison was to be at once removed. It was thought that the Pope might be obliged to fly, and now and then it was even foolishly suggested that he might go to America. Garibaldi was at work in the south of Italy. France, having concluded her war with Austria, was taking possession of Savoy. Sardinia was annexing Tuscany. The Roman police were repeatedly in collision with the people; and I was witness to at least one encounter when more than a hundred persons were wounded. The excommunication of Victor Emmanuel was decided on; and a few weeks later I saw it placarded on the doors of St. Peter's.

In 1868, I had another private interview with Pius IX. in company with the late George Peabody, for whom it was arranged by Mr. Hooker. Age had made its mark on him in the interval; and the conversation turned principally on works of charity and philanthropy, for which Mr. Peabody had become so celebrated. He bade us both sit down, and exhibited great interest in asking about Mr. Peabody's age, and in learning the extent of his benefactions, readily assenting to the suggestion that he should add his autograph to several fine imperial photographs of himself, and writing a sentence of the Bible upon three of them for Mr. Peabody, of which one was for me, and is now in my possession.

At both the periods above mentioned, I was again formally presented to his Holiness with the ladies of my party on Palm Sunday, and was uniformly impressed with the grace, dignity, and eminent benignity of his appearance and manner. I saw him also at a distance, in great ceremonials at St. Peter's, when the pomp and paraphernalia seemed as oppressive to him as they were to all beholders. If he was artful, as was sometimes said by his enemies, he had certainly acquired the "ars celare artem." He looked simple, humble, devout.

Not so ANTONELLI, with whom I was closeted twice in the little room next to the reception-room, in which "Chastity triumphing over temptation" is the subject of a large and very suggestive German picture. He was a person of great fascination for man or woman, with an eye of fire, and an affability of the most seducing sort. One needed not to be with him an hour to understand that everything at Rome, religious and secular, hinged on him, though he was adroit enough to make the Pope feel that his part as Premier was merely ministerial. He seemed the very impersonation of intrigue, political and social, with ability and *habilité* equal to any emergency.

Among other cardinals I met were BEDINI, who had come over as a legate to the United States, and whom I knew at that time, and ALTIERI, for whom I conceived a high opinion as an amiable and accomplished person. The latter nobly exposed himself in taking care of the poor during a cholera panic.

I remember hearing Père HYACINTHE preach eloquently at the French church in Rome. He afterward passed two or three days with me at Brookline, since he made so bold a stand against Ultramontanism and Papal Infallibility. One of the most interesting conversations I ever listened to occurred at my own table between him and Louis Agassiz, on the subject of the unity of the human race and the Bible history of creation. He impressed me as a modest, amiable man, with a good deal of genius, much earnest faith, and great eloquence, but with hardly energy enough to take the lead in a new Reformation.

I paid several visits to Rome at long intervals; and though my time there was chiefly devoted to art, I had opportunities of mingling in society at some great houses. I recall, in particular, a splendid entertainment given by Prince DORIA on the marriage of his daughter, and brilliant receptions at the Colonna Palace, where the Duc de GRAMMONT, the Comte de SARTIGES, and the Marquis de NOAILLES were successively in official residence as Ambassadors of France. The recent death of the hospitable and much lamented wife of my compatriot and friend, the sculptor STORY, has reminded me how often I have been privileged to meet distinguished or agreeable people in their spacious apartment in the Barberini Palace.

Of local Italian celebrities, the two I knew best were that accomplished scholar and profound student of Dante, the blind Duke of SERMONETA, and the eminent archæologist, VISCONTI, who was kind enough to point out to me in person numerous objects of interest, and to explain many curious things not within reach of the ordinary tourist. Sermoneta was head of the great house of Caetani, the most ancient of the Roman nobility; but this did not prevent him from being a leader of the progressive party, with a much greater love for exquisite design than for old forms and faiths, and with eyes wide open to everything new in literature and government. No greater contrast could be imagined than that which existed between him and the head of another great Roman family to whom I owed much kindness, Prince MASSIMO, the alleged descendant of Fabius Maximus, intelligent, accomplished, but full

of superstitious reverence for traditions, and an un-
questioning devotee of the Papacy. I sometimes
thought that a compromise of their two natures and
characters would make the best type of a Roman
citizen in those days.

Far the most interesting man I met during my first
visit to Florence, in 1860, was the blind GINO CAPPONI,
alike distinguished as a scholar and a patriot, whose
ancestor of the same name in the Middle Ages had also
been a leader of the popular party.

I have mentioned having seen the excommunication
of VICTOR EMMANUEL placarded on the outer walls of
St. Peter's. He soon afterward entered Florence in
triumph, and I was presented to him at a ball at the
Pitti Palace. I met him seven years later at an entertainment given by the municipality of Florence in honor
of the marriage of Prince Humbert and the beautiful
Princess Marguerite of Savoy. A man of coarse mould
and coarser habits of life, Victor Emmanuel looked gal-
lant and brave as Cæsar, impatient of all observances
and conventionalities, and sometimes breathing defiance
to all about him. In the ball-room at the Pitti, hedged
around by officers and ladies of his court, he seemed
like a wild boar at bay. But he had a great part to
play; and he played it with more moderation than
might have been expected from such a purely animal
nature. Amadeus, his second son, who died after having been for a short time King of Spain, whom I saw
at the head of a tournament, gave pleasing indications of intelligence and modesty, and exhibited both
gallantry and grace.

I had a piece of rare good-fortune in seeing CAVOUR at Turin in 1860. Madame de Circourt had given me a note to him, and I found him just forming a new Cabinet of which he had been appointed Premier. As he could not receive me at the moment, he wrote at once to invite me to the Foreign Office the next morning, where I spent an hour with him. He was most cordial and charming, and gave me a full impression of one whose loss to Italy was to be irreparable, as indeed it soon proved to be, for he died in the following year, leaving no one who could adequately supply his place.

With him I close the list of Continental celebrities whom I have known. As I look back upon my acquaintance with them, CAVOUR seems to me to have been, all things considered, the wisest and greatest of them all.

www.ingramcontent.com/pod-product-compliance
Lightning Source LLC
Chambersburg PA
CBHW022141020726
47496CB00008B/2493